Souls of Her Daughters

MALA NAIDOO

Publisher: Mala Naidoo
website: malanaidoo.com

First published in Australia 2018
This edition published 2018
Copyright © Mala Naidoo 2018
Cover design, typesetting: WorkingType (www.workingtype.com.au)

Naidoo, Mala
Souls of Her Daughters
ISBN- 978-0-6481377-1-9

pp246

ABOUT THE AUTHOR

Mala Naidoo lives in Australia with her family. She was born in South Africa during the apartheid era which is the impetus for her imaginative stories that take on a life of their own when the creative muse beckons. From a young age, Mala immersed herself in reading novels, plays, and poems from writers of the English literary canon through to contemporary writers. She has worked as a teacher in South Africa and Australia. Each novel, play or poem read, continues to enhance and receive her respect for the inspiration drawn from the artistry of the craft. This made Mala seek a space in this vast oasis of story-telling. Mala believes literature speaks through the values and culture of its characters, instilling understanding when readers connect to a moment in time, an event or conversation that brings clarity to daily existence. *Souls Of Her Daughters* is Mala Naidoo's third novel.

For You, For Me, For Us

If light is in your heart,
you will find your way home
~ Rumi

1

Friday Nights

Running through the carpark had become an unthinking act Grace engaged in for as long as she could remember. Stepping up her pace did nothing to warm her on this bitter night. She pulled her cardigan closer as she entered the building. Bright lights, a strong smell of high density disinfectant, pale grey walls and regulation blue flooring offered her the safety she craved, away from curious eyes.

The early part of Friday evenings was slow during the colder months at the Emergency Room at City Hospital. After the stroke of midnight, all hell would break loose.

Andrew Lang, tall, handsome intern with a pearly white smile and a twinkle in his eye, was every nurse's and doctor's catch. He sauntered towards Grace.

'Another deceptive start to the night, Grace. What's your prediction for tonight – busy or quiet?'

He was the only intern who addressed her by her first name, to the others Grace was always, 'Dr. Sharvin.'

'Who knows, Friday nights are never quiet. As always, I hope the injuries are minor and everybody leaves with their lives intact.'

Grace was average height, slim, with large, hazel brown eyes that glowed against her tanned skin, giving her a stunned, 'deer in the headlights' look. Her, long, soft, loosely curled, dark hair, tied in a tight knot, revealed her flawless skin. Her youthful glow belied her forty-five years.

She never smiled.

Her private life was a guarded vault.

'Any plans for your day off tomorrow?' Andrew Lang asked.

'I plan to sleep in before working on my paper for the conference. I'm a tad nervous I might not be as prepared this time.'

'You are thorough and offer extensive, relevant research, you will blow them away. Can I coerce you into having breakfast with me when we get off shift?'

Andrew's relentless invitations to breakfast, dinner, the museum, or a drive to the mountains never ceased to puzzle her. With almost fifteen years between them and his charm and good looks, he had a line-up of admirers waiting for a glance in their direction, yet he followed her around, hanging onto every word she said.

'I'm sorry, I have to decline, I'm ready to drop; I need my beauty sleep. After a Friday night on shift; my appetite is the furthest thought on my mind.'

'Next time, perhaps…' He smiled his pearly, flash of a smile to conceal his disappointment. 'See you on the other side of midnight, Dr. Sharvin!'

'See you later Dr. Lang, you should have an early dinner while things are slow.'

'Care to join me?' He asked with that well-known twinkle in his eye.

'You go on, I'll finish off my reports first.' Grace enjoyed the attention, she found the chase exciting and intended to keep it that way.

*   *   *

At 12:30 p.m., all hell broke loose, Grace received a telephone call to prepare for casualties coming in after a brawl outside a pub in Sydney's CBD.

Blaring sirens, blinding, flashing lights and the screeching halt of tyres meant the night at City Hospital emergency facility had to be ready for an ambush of physical traumas.

She shut her eyes, said a silent prayer and braced herself for what the night was about to become.

Paramedics wheeled in a young woman.

'Dr. Sharvin, twenty-four year old, pregnant female, bleeding after being kicked in the stomach and thrown down a flight of stairs. Forty-five year old male with head trauma,' the paramedic announced.

The young woman was silent, the man behind her had a large gash on his forehead, blood streamed down his face as he moaned, 'help me, help me, I only tried to help her, I can't see, I'm blind!'

The young woman slumped over. Grace rushed to her, calling out to Andrew Lang, 'attend to the male patient, clean up the head wound, assess how deep the gash is and suture if necessary. We need x-rays to determine if there are any fractures.'

The male patient's anxiety levels increased. He was a tall, thick-set man with a low pain threshold.

'My eyes, my eyes, I can't see, help me, please, my head hurts, please.'

Grace spat out instructions with mechanical ease, 'administer 2 mg Diazepam before you clean up his wound.'

The young woman she attended to, appeared unconscious, blood trickled down her legs, and her eyes were half-shut as she wafted in and out of semi-consciousness.

Grace called out, 'Nurse Hobbs, I need a heartbeat, please I need an ultrasound stat!' Grace maintained formality in her department, she addressed staff by their job titles to maintain professionalism which often fell by the wayside in this busy trauma unit.

Beth Hobbs, a young female intern, self-absorbed and lacking initiative, lifted the young woman as she loosened her clothes and proceeded with the ultrasound,

'Dr. Sharvin, no heartbeat from the foetus.'

'Keep trying Hobbs, there has to be a heartbeat, keep trying!' Grace was agitated, unlike her cool, unwavering professionalism, the hallmark of her personality as City Hospital head.

She hooked the cardiac machine on the young pregnant mother when her pager beeped.

A burn victim, an elderly woman was being shuttled in from a neighbouring suburb. Her obsession with candles caused a minor house fire.

Grace frantically applied the defibrillator to the young woman who was now unresponsive and lifeless – a pale, gaunt figure that Grace was desperate to awaken.

'Dr. Sharvin! Dr. Sharvin, the burn victim has arrived!'

'Nurse Hobbs, attend to the burn victim, I have to get this heart going, ring Dr. Romero; we need another medic on site tonight.'

City Hospital, in south-western Sydney, was grossly understaffed. Dr. Grace Sharvin covered most weekend night shifts. She was expected to carry the role of two doctors as head of the unit.

She looked at the young woman whose shallow breath began

to rise, her heart rate increased — Grace took in a deep breath, stepped aside and waited for Nurse Beth Hobbs to confirm if she was able to detect a heartbeat from the unborn child.

'No movement, I'm afraid, Dr. Sharvin.' Grace felt her own heartbeat quicken, *dear merciful god, what happened here? If this young woman pulls through, how will she cope? She is eight months into the pregnancy. She is already mother to her unborn child- how would she bear this?* Grace had to shake her sinking despair, she had to remain calm.

'Send her in for an emergency C-Section, we have to get the baby out to try to stimulate a heartbeat.'

Grace picked up the telephone to relay the urgency to theatre staff. All clinical signs indicated the baby was dead.

She walked over to Andrew Lang who had his patient stabilised, the wound was dressed and the patient was wheeled off for an x-ray.

The elderly woman was attended to and was to be sent home within the hour. Beds were scarce at City Hospital, patients who needed to be monitored had to lie in crowded holding areas, with no privacy to salvage their dignity, like livestock awaiting slaughter. Grace battled with the hospital board for many years for more staff, supplies, and space.

Nobody listened, she considered whether negligence to the glaring need was related to the location of the hospital or downright political inertia.

*   *   *

Grace locked herself in the ladies' room to catch her emotional breath. After many years of heading ER, she always ended up an emotional wreck, when a patient did not make it back home.

She washed her face, breathed deeply, trying to pull herself together. The night was young yet, nobody knew what else the sliding doors at ER would invite that night.

Andrew Lang walked to the ladies' room and knocked on the door,

'Grace, you okay? Are you unwell?'

Grace walked out, head held high, 'what makes you think, I'm unwell?'

'I caught a glimpse of you rushing out, I thought… you… might have been… unwell, sorry, I was just concerned…'

She pushed past him, ignoring his awkward hesitation.

Grace shielded herself in vulnerable moments with an impenetrable chilly disposition. Inner strength surfaced with a meanness that sent a shiver down the well-meaning Andrew Lang's spine.

The night brought in drunken young men involved in fist fights — these injuries were minor, one broken arm was as serious as the night got thereafter. A few car accident victims with cuts and burns filled up the evening.

She checked on the progress of the caesarean, and was glad the young woman was in recovery. She was strangely relieved that she did not have to let the woman know that the baby she was anticipating, was dead.

It was dark at 6 a.m. as she strolled to her car after a ten hour night shift. Her mind triggered the urgency to speed up her step, her body resisted from exhaustion as her thoughts danced off, a million miles away.

'See you on Monday, Grace,' she heard a subdued Andrew Lang say behind her.

'Yes, see you early on Monday evening, thank you, you were great last night in how you handled the distraught victim. Who knows what led to this situation tonight.'

Andrew lapped up his rare moment of acknowledgment. 'Thank you Grace, have a restful day.'

2

Dreams

The therapeutic value of sleep evaded Grace's weary body and disturbed mind. Her thoughts lingered on the woman who had lost her baby in a senseless attack. This played over several times in her head, leaving her more fatigued than she had ever been after her shift.

She showered, set her alarm, sent a text message to Patience to confirm their 7:30 p.m. dinner catch-up on her trip to Melbourne, and attempted to take a nap.

A fitful sleep ensued. Between a sleeping and waking state, she heard sounds from the street waft up to her apartment, a police siren and screeching car tyres soon faded as she drowsed off.

She hurried to her car on this cold wet night. The lone walk made her uneasy; the open-air carpark lay a distance away from the hospital gates. She was too weary to walk any faster.

7

She paused when she heard the tapping of hard-heeled shoes, with a missed beat on the second tap, behind her. Her blood warmed as she quickened her pace, the soles of her feet ached from many hours of standing through her busy shift. The hard-heeled walker whistled… she knew the tune…. She had the urge to look back, but walked faster, sensing the need to run…

Grace woke up with a jolt, choking as she drew a deep breath, got out of bed and walked to the lounge room, her favourite room in her apartment, with its large, downy couches that soothed and cradled her. The afternoon sun streamed through her apartment window. It made her drowsy, she nodded off for an hour.

Grace's east side of town, spacious eighth-floor, three-bedroom apartment had the amenities for a busy, single, professional woman – secure undercover parking, rooftop swimming pool, twenty-four hour gym and convenience stores on the ground floor. She paid off her mortgage six months after her mother passed away. She missed having her mother's round, smiling face greet her whenever she returned from her night shifts. Varuna's tragic car accident scarred Grace more than she admitted. A speed maniac shot out of his lane with no sign. Her car was airborne with the impact, plunging headlong, into the Georges River. She died of a heart attack before her car

hit the water. She looked forward to her monthly book club meetings in Gymea. They spent twenty wonderful, mother-daughter years together in Australia.

Grace took up further study in her first two years in Australia, to bring herself up to speed with Australian medical expectations. She received recognition for her dedication and contribution to medicine, with a rapid promotion to Head of the Emergency Unit at City Hospital. She presented papers on her research at medical conferences around the country and had written several journal articles on women's health issues. These opportunities inspired her to do more without the hindrance of sexism pecking at her self-confidence. She lived and breathed being a medical doctor with tenacious passion.

It kept her isolated.

Occasionally, her mother's sister visited from South Africa which always created tension in Grace's world. Her aunt would hound her about being unmarried. The relentless questions on why she did not have a 'nice young man' in her life and 'there had to be an eligible doctor' that she could marry. The comments irked her, whenever she heard them; implying she should marry a doctor according to the unwritten family decree. Nobody else was acceptable. She detested the snobbery and social status imposed upon her.

Grace recalled the words of her aunt. As she rose to make a cup of coffee, she mimicked the unmistakable lines that assaulted her ears over the years, *Darl, no nice young man in the whole of Australia?* No sooner had she uttered these infamous words, a wave of guilt engulfed her. A trip to South Africa to represent her mother's love for her ailing sister had to be committed to. She was the only family who had not given up on them. Grace vowed never to return to South Africa, on that final voyage to Sydney with her tearful mother, and an excited Patience two decades ago.

Her kitchen was a clinical museum, compared to her mother's warm, aromatic kitchen, with her amazing Indian and Thai inspired dishes. Her spin on everything she cooked from spicy grilled salmon with cashew nut sauce, chilli eggplant, and cumin potatoes, were delectable 'Varuna favourites'.

Grace pondered whether she should cook a curried chicken dish which Patience would appreciate after a few days away from home. She dispensed with that thought as she hadn't replenished her Indian spices since Varuna's passing. Her mother was a traditionalist in cooking Indian food. She roasted whole spices and ground them herself, believing additives destroyed the potency of the spice when pre-packaged and left to sit on shelves for years. Grace decided a bread and butter pudding after dinner, back at her apartment was an easier option.

She stepped out onto her balcony, the air was icy as the night before, it sent a shiver down her back. The street below bustled with activity as people rushed about their Saturday shopping – she avoided crowds and preferred shopping late at night, on her days off, to have the supermarket to herself. Many weekends spent locked in her apartment, reading, preparing for conferences or articles she had committed to writing, shut her off from the world. Watching old films her mother enjoyed was her preferred relaxation. Even as a child, she had an old head on her shoulders, her aunt never failed to remind her that her opinions should be kept to herself! Her mother's liberated view of life left her sister rolling her eyes and clicking her tongue at what Grace was permitted to do. Varuna's traditional side was exclusive to her culinary skills. She embraced anything new with great enthusiasm while maintaining her dignity and decorum.

Grace felt blessed that her mother and Patience had the opportunity to enjoy the beauty and freedom of living in Australia, a land that brought them joy and peace with their new-found anonymity.

She contemplated the past more so these days. The pace and intensity of the Emergency Room buffered her from slipping into a depressive state. She wished she could spend more time with Patience who understood her highs and lows. They shared a bond that few comprehended in the old country.

She knew she had to shrug her reverie if she hoped to complete her paper in time for the conference in Amsterdam. She toyed with the thought of tempting Patience into accompanying her on her week-long conference. They needed a holiday after their hectic year.

In a sunny corner of the lounge room, Grace logged into her computer and read through her last set of notes:

Women with physical trauma heal from the injury to the body, it's the soul, the psyche that harbours the injury for a lifetime if there is no intervention…

She worked through for two hours when she realised she had not eaten a morsel. Raisin toast and a pot of coffee would tide her over until dinner. She grabbed a bag of nuts to crunch her way through the next round of research.

The young woman who lost her child last night, surfaced in her thoughts, she made a note to follow through on the woman's recovery, and if possible, she would add this to her paper as a 'live' study. She had two months to complete her paper.

Her mobile phone intruded upon her thoughts. Patience's perennial chirpy voice greeted her.

'Hey Gracie, I've just landed, make sure you're on time, I'm starving!'

'I have an hour before you get out of the airport to the restaurant, I'll finish my work and see you soon!'

Grace adhered to punctuality at work, she often arrived late at dinner engagements with Patience, finishing off research or saving her work in multiple places. There was a quiet acceptance of each other's idiosyncrasies with Patience teasing Grace whenever she became too serious about the state of the world. She slapped a dollop of moisturiser on her tired face, stared at herself in the mirror, noticing with a tinge of sadness, the first fine lines that had taken residence on her forehead. Pulling her fringe over the lines and grabbing her coat, she hurried to her car.

Deserted carparks made her nervous, her South African wariness lingered with an unshakeable vengeance.

12

3

Sisterhood

Patience waited at their favourite table at *Thai Delight*. She dressed for the middle of summer. Her braided hair bounced about her shoulders. Patience, too, had a youthful look, she guarded her age with fierce privacy often dropping off a few years or adding on a few if she needed to garner attention or respect from the company she was in. Her yellow suit made her the brightest person in the room. She had no reservations about how much *bling* she wore, often saying to Grace, 'I will teach you to shine girl!'

Grace rushed towards Patience's outstretched arms, she rose to her feet bearing a smile that lit up the Thai diner. They drew curious glances wherever they went.

'Gracie, so good to see you! What have you been getting up to while I was out of town? Working, working, working, I know!'

'Hey sis, I missed you and it's only been four days!' Grace laughed, her steel guard melted around Patience.

'Yes, no one to nag you to get out and about, eat and sleep right?'

'Yeah, you know the drill, tell me, what's the latest, what did you take away from the conference?'

'Let that wait for a while girl, I need Thai Delight tonight! What about you, you're wasting away, I was not around to feed you and a famine struck, and it's only been four days!' Patience had a deep, husky laugh that made anyone within earshot smile.

'Stop that Patience, you exaggerate! Now, we have everybody looking in our direction.'

'Grace, the same girl as always, hiding away. Enough of that, I want a round of those curry puffs and chicken satay to start. How about you? Let me warn you, I could eat a horse — those minuscule finger foods at the conference were a little too dainty for my appetite! I was going to ask you to cook your magical chicken curry, but, knew you had a busy Friday night so my sympathy kicked in!'

'Well let's settle for a feast tonight, I'll have the same starters you're having.'

'We've been together too long, we are turning into an old married couple, soon we'll be finishing each other's sentences! Heaven forbid!'

Patience never failed to lighten the mood, she had been Grace's anchor without realising it. They spent their childhood years together ever since Patience's mother, Mama Elsie, arrived to assist Varuna in the care of her ailing mother. Grace's family were fourth generation Indian living in South Africa. It was Varuna's unwritten duty that she would care for her mother until the end of her days. Nursing homes invited community gossip which Varuna avoided; Grace upheld this in her duty to her mother. Mama Elsie and Patience stayed on as part of the Sharvin family when Grace's maternal grandmother died. Patience was four years old, three years younger than Grace when they met.

Patience's family hailed from the outskirts of Kwa-Zulu Natal. She imbibed the culture and values of the Sharvin home and shared the values Mama Elsie taught her. A country that operated on a divide and rule ideology could not quell the multiculturalism in their home. She trained as a social worker with Grace's financial backing and support. Grace admired Patience's commitment in setting up safe houses for abused women in Victoria, South Australia, and New South Wales. It was her life's passion to protect and nurture women in distress.

'The best thing about the conference these past four days is that funding has been secured to set up another safe house in Western Australia, the businesswomen who attended, pledged enough to cover more than half the cost of the house I was keen on, a few months ago. More fundraising drives and our WA sisters will be in safe care. I'm stoked this dream is achievable now!'

Grace jumped up and hugged her, this was a mission Patience was hoping to make possible for the sisters.

'You're amazing in your tireless efforts, girlfriend! Mama Elsie would be so proud of all that you have achieved.'

'Yeah, she's beside me all the way, I have my quiet spiritual conversations with her when I need some direction on how to move forward. It spooks you when I say this, but I do get some signs that direct my actions after these conversations.'

'Not spooked, it's just not something I've experienced. I wish mum would speak in my dreams, even if it was to tell me she was in a good place, you know. I'm not sceptical at all.'

'Let's drop this serious stuff, what's your news, how's that dashing young intern, still following you around?'

'He's just a kid, I don't want to encourage him in any way. I must come across as some sort of 'Lady Macbeth!' Friday night was quiet to start with but something really threw me, a young woman who I hope you can bring into your care, came in after a violent assault, she was kicked down a flight of stairs. The thing is, she was in the last weeks of her pregnancy… we couldn't save the baby. She had an emergency C-section last night. I hope she will…' Her throat felt dry, she coughed to conceal her swelling emotions. She shook her head fighting off the turbulence within.

'You can't let this affect your equilibrium Grace, I know how difficult it must be and while you think you are 'Lady Macbeth' with that nice intern; you have a big, caring, but wounded heart. I will say it again and you can tell me to shut up, but, you need to continue the counselling sessions – you should not have stopped them after Mama Varuna passed on.'

Patience reached across the table touching Grace's hand, acknowledging the emotional baggage that only two women who were close, could share and understand.

'I know after dad's death and then mum… I will give it some thought, now tell me how's Felicity, did you get to spend much time together at the conference?' Grace found it difficult to talk about resorting to therapy to help her cope with her anxieties.

'Felicity and I were at the same hotel, she made a holiday of it as she does. We had breakfast together every morning, she's on a hectic schedule too, so many cases at the moment, a refugee issue has arisen, this is keeping her on her toes and yet she gives her time and expertise to our *Women in Distress Campaign*. The statistics on the abuse of women in detention centres and state prisons is staggering, Felicity's support for the legal ramifications is essential. She sends her regards and might come over to Sydney late in October for a case here, she says she might extend her stay to get in some 'family time' with us.'

'That will be great, it's been months since I've last seen her, I'm responsible for not keeping in touch and always relying on you to keep me up to speed with things. I hope to catch up with her before I leave for Amsterdam. It will be good to go to Melbourne again. I hope you're working on taking time off to keep me company in Amsterdam.'

'Let Felicity know well in advance, not your usual last minute arrangements *Gracie,* and I'm sure you both can have a catch up. I'm not sure about Amsterdam though. You will be busy all day and the nights are filled with dinner parties. I always feel like an impostor attending those dinners.'

Grace laughed, she remembered how awkward Patience was at the last medical conference dinner. She sat smiling for the entire evening, trying to fit in, hoping nobody would ask her questions. Patience knew Grace like the back of her hand, always rushing around at the last minute in her personal life. She carried a lot of the work of others in her ER team.

After the spicy Thai meal, both indulged in a shared fried ice-cream dessert, a favourite they enjoyed. They headed back to Grace's apartment for coffee.

Grace drove into the underground parking, and frantically locked the doors when she saw a man alight from his car. She grew agitated when Patience reached to unlock the door.

'Wait a minute Patience, let him walk to the elevator first, we can chat in the car without him noticing us.'

'Grace, stop this, he is a harmless man. Does he live in the building? I don't suppose you would know. You can't go on living like this.'

Grace grabbed Patience's arm, begging her to wait awhile. Patience conceded with a loud clicking of her tongue, and slipped into a combination of Zulu and English,

'*Wena, eish, si'ssie,* you must get over this. You cannot live in perpetual fear, this is Australia!'

'You don't read the newspapers, a woman was accosted by a man on her way home from work; she struggled but managed to escape. Lots go unreported too.'

'I know, we have to be careful but not paranoid, Grace, you need to address this, you seem to have become tenser after Mama Varuna passed away. Please promise you will go back to your counsellor for both our sakes,'

'I will, I will, lets hurry to the apartment, he's gone now.'

They chatted until two in the morning. Grace convinced Patience to stay over. She conceded, to prevent Grace from stressing over her safety if she left at that unearthly hour.

Patience could not resist saying as she headed off to the guest room, 'Get a life, Gracie! And, never fear, I will be sampling some of your bread and butter pudding for breakfast!'

She laughed her husky, honeyed laugh, masking her concern for Grace's increasing inability to relax.

4

Memories

Grace was restless after Patience went to bed, she showered, crawled into bed and lay staring at the ceiling; she reached across to the bedside table and pulled her laptop onto the bed. If sleep was not possible, it was best to make use of this wakefulness. She had the next day off and hoped to get a fair bit prepared for her paper.

She heard footsteps on the corridor and voices on the balcony next door. It was a cold July evening, she wondered who would want to be outdoors on such a night. They would have to be smokers. New neighbours moved into the apartment next door, she had not crossed paths with them, two male voices wafted over. They had to be talking in raised voices if she could hear their mumble with her windows and balcony sliding door sealed. Being on edge, suspecting the worst of strangers added to her disturbed sleeping pattern.

Mrs. Beresford, her eighty-year-old neighbour, was away in Canada visiting her daughter. Varuna was a friendly neighbour who always looked in on Mrs. Beresford, taking her little treats each time she baked something. Grace's cautious nature led to conversations on why one should not take home-cooked delights to an elderly neighbour, what if she had allergies or a health condition that could kill her if she ate well-intentioned homemade treats. Varuna, much like Patience, teased Grace on her bleak predictions. Mrs. Beresford maintained her friendship with Grace, ringing to check on her after her mother's death. Although Varuna was in her seventies, she insisted on addressing Maryanne Beresford as, 'Mrs. Beresford,' as her mark of respect. Grace scrolled through photographs of her mother on her laptop, smiling when she remembered the mother-daughter banter on Varuna's formality of address with Maryanne.

'It's a cultural thing. I cannot call her Maryanne, she's a mother figure in my eyes.'

'Just as long as you don't expect me to call her *Aunty*, please mum.' Grace laughed and Varuna shook her head.

'I don't think I could stand it if you called me *Varuna* instead of mum.'

'Okay *Varuna*, I understand, I will maintain my roots,' Grace teased. Her mother's 'untraditional' ways never crossed the line of respect.

She missed her mother like an absent sunbeam on a rain soaked day. Age was no deterrent to their closeness, they did everything together, shared every angst and joy with Patience close in tow.

Grace's father ran his own busy wood yard business and often had to run deliveries himself to remote parts of Durban. Staff were unreliable and not to be trusted. He delivered a load of wood, early one Friday morning in Kwa-Mashu and never returned home. After three frantic days, his burnt out vehicle and charred remains were discovered in remote farmlands. Grace struggled with the news of her father's horrific murder. Her final year at school tested her coping mechanism, she threw herself into her studies to blunt her pain. Varuna kept the home together and took over the running of the wood yard until a year before they left for Australia. Her driving force was her wish, along with her husband, to ensure that Grace was educated and able to fend for herself. Studying to be a doctor was the only option, nothing else was considered suitable for a man who ran and worked in a wood yard. He wanted to say with pride, 'my Grace is a doctor.' He was a simple man with high aspirations for his only daughter.

After the passing of her father, interfering relatives stuck their chiselled, sticky beaks into Varuna's world, badgering her with questions, insisting on knowing whether she was 'a wealthy widow' to 'you must get Grace married off to a rich man.'

Grace resisted many offers of 'Indian-Victorian' arranged marriage proposals. This put tremendous pressure on Varuna to brush off unwanted offers, upholding that marriage had to be her daughter's choice. Grace referred to her father's family as the 'outlaws' who brought hordes of prospective husbands to her home, tall ones, short ones, fat ones, skinny ones, acne ravaged ones, ones with a barrel of hair gel on their glistening heads, and ones that looked old enough to be her father. After a dozen such attempts, Varuna barred all prospective suitors her in-laws encouraged, this severed all ties with the 'outlaws.'

Grace remembered Patience saying in true Zulu tradition they would have to slaughter an animal as ritualistic thanks for not securing a *walrus looking* husband! Much laughter brought Varuna to the room, joining in on the merriment. Mama Elsie would watch Varuna giggling with the girls, shaking her head and smiling her quiet, unspoken views on the situation. Elsie reminded Patience that her place in the Sharvin house was that of domestic staff. Once when Patience became distant and quiet, Grace urged her for the reason for her behaviour and Varuna ironed out the situation with Elsie by simply saying, 'Patience is my child as you are my sister, accept that Elsie, *please.*' She slipped into speaking Zulu when she spoke to Elsie on matters of grave concern.

Their household of four women courted much gossip about their living arrangement. Patience attended the same school as Grace which was legally prohibited but not enforced in the Sharvin home – apartheid got a kick in the pants on that score!

Grace graduated from high school and began her medical studies. She worked many weekend hours to save as much as she could for Patience's tertiary studies. Her mother had too many financial burdens to bear with the slow decline of the wood yard business. She was determined they would leave South Africa as soon as she secured a medical position overseas. Their unspoken promise was, never to commit to a man unless they had his utmost respect.

She eventually fell asleep with the memories of a time past.

*　　*　　*

She walked to her car at a slower pace to avoid slipping into a puddle during this unseasonable downpour. She heard foot-steps behind her, she quickened her pace — the walkway to the carpark was long and narrow. Grace moved over to the left of the walkway, the wet grass along the borders of the pathway squished under her soft shoes.

She crept further to the edge when the footsteps grew louder, to allow the passer-by space to get ahead of her. The person began to hum… a familiar tune… A tall figure, in a hooded rain jacket, passed her, she felt a gush of cold air hit her with the fast pace of the walker. The figure stopped, sniffed the surrounding air – she felt his face on her shoulder and then… his nose on her arm, sniffing like a beast… she froze in her steps – a muffled male voice said, 'nice perfume.' The rain pummelled down, her legs were wet; her feet were icy. She felt like running back to the hospital, her knees caved in, she fell onto the sodden ground. Her tormentor hurried on. Struggling to stand up in the muddy slush, she stretched to find her mobile phone in her handbag. There was no reply from her mother, she called Patience, only to hear, 'You've reached Patience, please be patient and leave a message; I'll get back to you soon.' Patience's giggle at the end of the message infuriated her. Where were the two people she counted on when she needed them the most? She stopped, searching ahead for the lights of a departing car. Had the person left the hospital parking grounds?

As she got close to her car, she heard the faint lyrics of the hummed song… one she struggled to recall. The song grew louder as she got closer.

Grace gasped, bathed in sweat as she came up for air, she yelped when she felt a crick in her neck.

She walked to Patience's door and stopped, feeling guilty that Patience had had an exhausting few days and deserved a restful sleep. Much was left unresolved in her life, perhaps Patience was right; she needed closure. She was mourning her mother's death, a year later, and uninvited ghosts from her past resurfaced.

Her thoughts flitted to the young woman who was brought into ER on Friday night. Something nagged at her to act on her instincts, to follow up on the patient's wellbeing. She made a note on her iPhone to call the hospital admin on how the young woman was doing. This thought quelled the horror of the nightmare that disturbed her sleep.

She needed a dose of Patience's good sense and relentless humour to break down the walls of her fear. After hours of restless contemplation, she fell into a light sleep on the couch, her refuge from troubled sleep.

5

Cultural Command

Patience grew up on the outskirts of Pietermaritzburg. Her parents, devout Christians, wanted the best for their only daughter. Mama Elsie developed a uterine infection after Patience's birth, making her infertile. Both parents devoted all their energy, time and what little they had to ensure Patience had a comfortable life. Goodwin Mkhize attended Sunday morning services at the local community church in a run-down building, packed with earnest worshippers. His death at the hands of an unknown assailant, on his return home, after a euphoric sermon, cast suspicion on speculated enemies of the church.

After her husband's death, Elsie had to fend for herself. Goodwin left her penniless, the businessman, he worked for, paid him a pittance with no superannuation or death benefits. She spent many months scouring through tossed out daily newspapers for job vacancies. Whenever she visited the local general-dealer stores to check the classified section for employment opportunities, business owners cast their beady eyes on her, assuming her ploy was to steal something, and some would throw her out.

She discovered she could read the newspaper at the local library without being thrown out, the irritation was that she was watched by suspicious librarians, peering above the rims of their glasses, racism visible in their eyes.

Elsie, a tall, slender woman with light skin, and grey, almond-shaped eyes was fluent in English. Her soft, lilting accent made her an anomaly in her tribe – some members viewed her as the friend of white folk, a sell-out in the fight for democracy. She had no hope of becoming a medical reception-ist, a role she desired, not in a country that saw black women as limited to performing menial domestic chores — nothing more. She applied for the housekeeper position with the Shar-vin family. She feared her four-year-old daughter would be a deterrent to acquiring the job, when her employer realised her child would be at work with her. The interview with Varuna Sharvin was more than Mama Elsie imagined, she heard many stories about applicants being bullied and ridiculed during the interview. The warmth and respect, she received from Varuna made her believe she was guided by her prayers to this family. A furnished bedroom in the family home and meals taken with the family was more than she had expected. She had to upkeep the home while Varuna nursed her ailing mother.

Patience was a shy little girl, awkward and in awe of her new home. Both mothers ran an organised household with Grace's father's rigid bedtime rule for children. Patience had to be bathed and in bed, reading by seven-thirty on weeknights. Her indigenous heritage accentuated her difference at school, making her retreat into alienated silence until Grace stepped in, in the role of 'protective older sister,' putting an end to bullying or situations that would make Patience uncomfortable.

Two little girls grew in love and warmth as the early reminders that difference based on race was of no consequence.

Their mothers grew in trust and friendship.

Several happy years passed until Elsie's death from a debilitating bout of pneumonia. Lack of medical attention during her childhood struggle with asthma had weakened her lungs.

Patience was still in mourning when two men, dressed in traditional attire with cow tails on their arms and legs, arrived early, one Sunday morning. The older of the two addressed Varuna,

'Good morning Mama, we are here to take our daughter, Patience, back home where she belongs. The chief has issued this decree.'

Varuna did not invite them in as she did others who called at the house — she spoke to them from behind the security gate.

'Patience is my responsibility, this is her home. She is eighteen years old and cannot be taken against her will, I will not allow it.'

'Mama when the chief speaks, we have to carry out his wishes. We will be beaten if we do not take her back now.'

'What is your name, I will send a message to your chief.'

'But you can't, you are a *woman*, he won't accept your word. My name is Kagiso Dlamini. My name means 'peace', I come in peace, please Mama, please I beg you, send Patience with us, we fear for our lives.'

'Kagiso, I understand you are the messenger but please take my message back to your chief, Patience will be going **nowhere**, least of all with two strange men!'

The men left once they understood Varuna would not accept their demands.

When Varuna called the police, she clashed with their hostility.

'Sorry Mrs. Sharvin, we do not have control over tribal law and Patience Mkhize is a Zulu, technically you are breaching the law by forcibly keeping her in your home.'

Varuna tried in vain to explain her relationship with Patience when the telephone was plonked down on her. This was the situation her beloved husband found intolerable, the law gave them no representation.

She got much the same response from her family lawyer, with a shred of hope that he could put a three month hold on Patience being removed from their home. He advised Varuna to move out of the family home and remain in hiding until the situation calmed down. Patience limited her movements, afraid she would be kidnapped by the chief's henchmen.

Their peaceful lives were shattered by the threat of separation.

Grace was in her fifth year at medical college in Durban, she worked part-time at a local pharmacy on her weekends in Pietermaritzburg to fund Patience's university education to achieve her dream of being a social worker.

Varuna left the house for Johannesburg at 4 a.m. with Patience sprawled low in the backseat, sweating under several heavy blankets. They had to keep moving until things settled in Pietermaritzburg. Grace had plans to secure a medical position in rural New South Wales as new doctors were being touted to staff hospitals in the country.

They moved from one motel to another across the country, avoiding entry into Kwa-Zulu Natal in fear that Patience would be kidnapped. Varuna's assistant manager at the wood yard, Petros Sibaya, was a trusted employee. He was the eyes and ears of what the chief and his men were up to. Varuna told him to move into her house while she and Patience were on the run. He refused, saying it would make the chief's men and the police suspicious about their activities.

One evening after moving to the seventh motel, Patience spoke up.

'Mama Varuna, I can't expect you to continue doing this. You are separated from Grace and I know she misses seeing you, please lets abandon this and go back home. Whatever happens, I will not stop loving you and Grace.'

'Patience, that is the silliest thing I've heard you say, Grace knows this is necessary to keep our family intact, this is temporary. Your mother, may God rest her soul, would not want you to give up. I'm so glad we could register you with Open Universities to study while we are on the move.'

'I feel awful that you are separated from Grace and I hate being locked away as we are.'

'Look it's a wet day, everybody will be indoors at home, let's go out to a movie tonight, I know how cooped up you've been.'

'That will be wonderful! What would you like to see? I don't mind, just to be out is all I need.'

Varuna decided that dinner and a movie was what Patience needed to shake her maudlin mood.

The hired car had a tank of petrol ready for a getaway at short notice. They set off earlier to do some shopping before the movie. An early, relaxed pizza dinner at *Casalottis'* for a healthy cauliflower base pizza was their choice.

'I have put on weight with this cloak and dagger life now, Mama, that's why I need more clothes. This pizza is indulgent but a healthy indulgence at least.'

'Talk about you, look at me! We have to exercise, Patience. Damn that chief, whoever he is, for mucking up our lives. We have to look after ourselves.'

The joy of being out and about after living in the shadows for several weeks, allowed them to relax.

'I think we can return home soon, Petros says, according to his inside source, there are no rumblings from the chief's men.'

'I hope so, I miss Grace. Let's stop at the ladies' room before we head to the movies.'

'You go ahead I'll browse around here and wait for you.'

*   *   *

An hour later Patience had not returned from the ladies' room.

Varuna regretted not going with her. She felt sick with worry; she called the police, called Grace and walked to the ladies' room, hoping and praying she would appear.

Patience was gone.

She left her handbag with Varuna… her mobile phone rang inside the bag. She picked it up, the line was dead.

Varuna lay in bed that night praying for Patience's safety, 'Lord, please keep my child safe and return her soon. I was foolish in thinking Johannesburg was a safe option. I should have hired a bodyguard. Please deliver her to us no later than by morning.' She was always direct in whatever she did, even when praying.

Her frenzied mind, consumed by fear, refused to accept that women who disappeared, never returned.

6

Searching

Grace arrived in Johannesburg to assist Varuna in locating Patience. They were both aware that without telephone contact in this overcrowded metropolis, it would be searching in a veritable haystack.

Varuna was inconsolable upon seeing Grace, her fears could not be contained any longer. They knew if Patience was snatched by anyone other than the chief, the chance that she was dead, was a possibility. Grace had to assume the lead as her mother's fragility had taken hold of her reason.

'Mum, you have to remain calm, we have to put our heads together to figure out whether Patience was taken by strangers or whether she ran off of her own volition.'

'How can you say that Grace? She is *your sister*... she would not do that! She is my responsibility and... and... I promised her mother... ' Varuna stopped unable to make eye contact with Grace.

'Mum, you said she was distressed about being in hiding; that she felt awful about us not being together. Is there anything I should know, any leads to finding Patience?'

'No, she would not run off. I have always tried to be open with both of you. What do you mean by asking if there is anything you should know? There are no secrets...' Varuna broke off, a sudden burst of perspiration covered her brow and upper lip.

'Could she perhaps have met a young man while you both have been on the hop from town to town, motel to motel? I found it difficult keeping tabs on where you both were from one week to the next.'

'That is not possible, we were together all the time. This was the first time we were separated when she went to the ladies' room. She asked me to go with her. I let her down!' Varuna accepted guilt for everything that went awry in their lives. Her tears could not dry when her heart bled for Patience's safety.

'You both probably felt safe, it's natural to drop one's guard.'

'It was my suggestion to get out. Patience was feeling boxed-in and anxious about our separation from you. The police are apathetic and throw statistics at me. Nobody has been appointed to investigate the case. Each time I call, I'm put through to a different officer. One female officer had the audacity to ask if Patience was my maid and whether she ran off because she did not want to work for me anymore. They have no idea what our relationship is like. Damn this country! Its politics has made people inhumane.'

'We are victims in this crazy place. We have to leave for Australia as soon as my final internship is over. We have to find Patience.'

'I admire your determination, but there's something, I have

not spoken about before… it's time to reveal what has been kept in the dark… hear me out on this.'

Grace looked at her mother, petrified of what was to follow.

'What is it? Has Patience run away then?

'No, no, far from it! Do you remember when Mama Elsie was very ill, Mr. Cooppan, the lawyer, came to see her?'

'Yes, I never really asked any questions back then. Is there a problem?'

'Not a problem but information both you and Patience need to be aware of. Mama Elsie asked me to legally adopt Patience before she passed away. She was terrified the chief would come to claim her at some stage. He apparently declared, when Patience was born, that when she reached puberty she would be his wife. Patience's parents lived in fear of that day. The lawyer said if I legally adopted her and she bore the 'Sharvin' surname, the chief would have no binding tribal hold on Patience.'

'The suspense is killing me, I hope you agreed to legally adopt her… *mum*… out with it please!'

'Patience Sharvin is your sister, my daughter in the eyes of the law and in my heart. I planned to tell you both when we were preparing our applications for Australia. We have to find your sister, Grace.'

'How could you keep this from us? Why?'

'It's complicated, I had to honour Elsie's love for her daughter, for Patience to understand that her mother's request was out of love for her, in her concern for her daughter's safety.'

'How did you manage her university application?'

'I did the online application and have been handling all email correspondence up to this stage.'

Grace hugged Varuna, they clung to the hope that Patience would return soon.

'I think I understand why you kept it from us, I know Patience will too.'

'I knew you would be happy to know that I honoured Elsie's wishes.'

'I lived in hope too, that this might happen. Patience became my sister the day she arrived at our home.'

'I had to proceed with caution, even if the law sanctioned the adoption, tribal customs seem to take precedence.'

'Now, my gut feeling is that you both were being watched. It could well be the chief that has taken Patience. We need to find out as soon as we can. I think we should tap into a few contacts in Pietermaritzburg to test my theory. I can only stay for a week, I have some hospital rounds to cover which is vital to me graduating.'

'You cannot put your studies on hold, I know how anxious you are to start our new lives abroad. Don't jeopardise your studies, you've come this far and must complete it.'

'I'm going to get you something to eat and then we'll go back to where you and Patience shopped and had dinner before she disappeared. Hopefully, we will get a sense of what really happened.'

'You could have been a detective, you used to say during your *Nancy Drew* reading craze that you wanted to be a private investigator for women.'

This moment of recollection made them smile for a brief moment.

'Trust you to have a mother memory in a moment of crisis!'

*   *   *

It was a cold, wet, miserable Saturday afternoon in downtown Johannesburg. The streets were grey, a sparse smattering of people rushed for shelter from the steady soaking rain. The streets were filthy — bins were overflowing, saturated paper bags were strewn on collapsing sidewalks, discarded plastic bags clogged drains or floated down overflowing gutters.

Grace and Varuna hurried to the shopping district where Patience was last seen.

'This part of the city is disgusting! When are people going to reduce their intake of fast food, its killing the

population? Let's hurry, the streets are deserted and we don't want to add to the crime statistics.'

'I can't walk any faster, the surface is slippery, hang onto my arm Grace. People eat fast food because it's what most can afford as their warm meal, I suppose.'

'I know, I see so many young people with health issues caused by malnutrition or poor eating habits. Being at the hospital has been an eye opener! You ensured we had healthy meals when I was growing up. You were very hard on me and my sweet tooth.'

'Well, that's why you still have your strong white teeth. I know you're thanking me now for my strict diet regime when you were a child,'

Grace gave her mother a loving nudge. She enjoyed being in company with Varuna. This time it was laced with dreaded fear and nebulous hope.

They walked to the ladies' room where Patience might have been last seen.

'Perhaps we can get access to surveillance footage of the ladies' room that might indicate whether Patience was taken.'

The shopping centre janitor was non-committal when they approached him, he shook his head and shrugged his shoulders at all questions asked. After an hour of running around the building, they located a tiny office next to the elevator on the ground floor. The shopping centre manager sat in a dingy room with the blinds down, avoiding contact with the public lest he was called upon to address problems that arose. They asked to see the footage from two days ago. After a lot of excuses about how long it would take and that the ladies should return in two days, Varuna slipped the man two hundred rands; soon he was scrolling through the day in question, beaming like one who had won the weekly lottery.

They saw scores of women enter and leave the ladies' room. Just as they were deciding to call it a day, Grace pointed to the screen,

'That's her walking towards the ladies' room, nothing untoward there. Please zoom in with a panning view of the area behind Patience,' Grace urged.

'This is police business, I'm not supposed to give you access to the surveillance footage, why do you want it anyway?'

'Have the police had a look at this footage since my daughter was reported missing? We have to take the law into our own hands if we hope to find her. This should not surprise you!'

'Your daughter? That was a black woman you pointed to,' he sneered.

'Are you being racist? Just do your job and zoom into the surrounding area.' Grace was livid that race was an issue, the first thing everybody was eager to highlight while neglecting important issues that needed attention.

There appeared to be nothing unusual except for two women who were leaning over the railings in conversation.

They watched on for a few more minutes when Patience was seen exiting the ladies' room in the direction she came from. One of the women at the railings walked up to her, appeared to say something to her, placed her arm on Patience's left arm and guided her out the building — Patience did not appear to resist, she glanced backwards which Grace was sure, was the silent acknowledgement that Varuna was waiting for her.

Grace and Varuna watched as Patience's image vanished out of view. The building manager refused to give them a copy of the footage, claiming he was not legally allowed to do that. Grace could not hold back her frustration,

'So it's legal to be *paid* to show us the footage but not legal to give us a copy?' She yanked her camera from her handbag and proceeded to photograph what she needed. They needed proof that Patience left with a woman who spoke to her outside the ladies' room.

The hypocrisy of selective values in this lawless land was the bane of her existence.

They had to continue with their own investigation if they hoped to see Patience again.

7

The Dreaded Day

An unrestricted day excited Patience. The crisis made Varuna over protective as she guarded her little family with eagle-eyed vigilance. They stopped social media activities, even though mother and daughter had doubts regarding the chief's attachment to online activities.

*　　*　　*

Rain provided a good decoy. People were less inclined to watch people on a dreary, rainy day in chilly Johannesburg. Patience draped a black scarf around her neck to haul over as a cover to keep her dry and inconspicuous from deliberate eyes. She wore a black jacket and a pair of black jeans for her incognito day out. Varuna tossed aside her colourful clothes and dressed in a grey jacket and long black skirt. Johannesburg was not a place Patience enjoyed visiting. She had childhood memories of listening to Friday night radio broadcasts of the serialised, *Squad Cars*. Blaring police sirens, a hail of bullets fired, dramatic music and a voice announcing,

The story you're about to hear is true. Details are supplied from the official case files by the South African police. Only names and places have been changed to protect innocent people involved.

Patience clung to Grace with fear and the thrill of criminals being apprehended. *Squad Cars* was a Friday night radio ritual in the Sharvin home, any child daring to ask questions in the middle of an episode, faced a warning look and risked instant dismissal to bed.

Patience looked forward to shopping for clothes, complaining that inactivity in the past months had pushed her up a notch in dress size. The only thing she enjoyed about Johannesburg was the variety of cuisine available to discerning taste-buds.

They enjoyed the stolen moments of freedom but bemoaned Grace's absence.

Forty-five minutes into the meal and twenty minutes before the movie, Patience went to the ladies' room.

She was mindful that she should not leave Varuna alone for too long.

The queue was long on this cold evening. Everyone sought refuge from the rain in the shopping centre. She kept her head down, eyes fixed on the ground, fearing being recognised by someone who might call out her name. She fastened the black scarf over her head, flattened her hair which was her pride and joy, she spent many hours at the local hair weaving salon, for that elaborate coiffed look. Varuna ensured Patience and Grace indulged their feminine needs even if it meant relinquishing something, she needed.

As she stepped out a woman called out, reaching for her arm, 'please miss, please help me, I can't find my son, I'm so worried someone has taken him.'

'That's awful, call the police, I have to go, someone is waiting for me.'

'Please miss, I asked so many people, everybody walks away. Nobody looks at me… please. I can't go home without my son, my husband will…'

Fear was visible in her eyes. She had to answer for the boy's disappearance.

'Let me bring the person waiting for me along, so we have more eyes looking out for your son.'

'No please, I know you won't come back, please you look like a kind person, please help me.'

Patience was annoyed for leaving her phone in her handbag, 'take me to the spot where you last saw your son. You must call the police, I'll have a quick look for you but I don't know your son, do you have a photograph of him? I have to hurry.'

The woman flashed a photograph of her son on her phone for Patience to have a quick look.

'I need to have a good look at his face, you pulled it away too soon.'

Patience held her hand before she could snatch the phone away.

She followed the woman into the elevator, it stopped in the basement of the parking lot, she turned to speak to the woman as they walked out – she felt someone grab her from behind, a thud to her head followed as her legs collapsed under her.

It was dark when she opened her eyes. The car was stationary, she heard the woman's muffled voice.

'I want my payment and my son, I did what you asked. She was easy, believed every word I said. She must love children, she looked very sad when I told her my son was missing. I must have seemed convincing. You should pay me extra for being a good actress too.'

A male voice with a deep, resonant, thick accent replied, 'you will get what we said you would receive *if you brought the 'package' from Jo-burg, not a cent more. Your child will remain here for a few days until we know you will not go to the police, understood!'

'No, please let me take my son with me now, he is afraid and will be looking for me, please, I have done what you wanted. I need the money.'

'You will stay in the women's quarters until we are sure you are not lying.'

She left with one of the chief's men. Patience kept her eyes shut, she had to feign sleep to avoid any physical abuse. She grew anxious as she thought of Varuna and Grace. *Did they go to the police? Was a search party out?* She sucked in the urge to sob, *who am I kidding? I am a black woman missing where people go missing in droves.* As this thought sunk in she knew she would never return home.

A short, skinny man dragged her out the car.

'Where am I?'

'You are home where you belong.'

Patience pricked up her ears, drumbeats and a pulsating clapping of hands floated across the warm night air; she turned to the sound, a large camp fire was glowing ahead. She squinted to clear her eyes, her head felt heavy. Figures dancing around the fire came into focus.

'Please put me down, there's no need to carry me, I can walk to wherever you are taking me,'

'No! I'm not stupid, we've come so far; I cannot let you run away now.'

'I cannot run away, I don't know where I am, trust me.'

'*Trust?* What is that? I trust no one!'

He trudged along with her until the dancing women were visible, twelve of them, around a rotund, aging man. He sat on an ornate, carved seat.

'You are at the kraal and kingdom of the chief of your tribe. You must go down on your knees to prostrate to him. All his wives have to do this.'

She was back in Kwa-Zulu Natal in the clutches of the chief and his band of genuflecting men and fawning wives. Her mother had told her the chief was a ruthless man. She glanced up at him. He struggled to breathe, his eyes were concealed in sagging folds of skin; his head swayed in a slow, mindless rhythmic motion to the beating drums. He seemed incapable of being a threat; it was his men she had to fear. She observed from her lowered position, old and young dancing around the fire in an emotionless trance.

She crawled towards the chief who was surrounded by at least twenty men, armed with spears and knives. The women broke out in a loud ululating as she approached the chief's feet. He raised his index finger and the eldest woman walked up to him, fell prostrate to the ground and rose with downcast eyes. She reached over and handed him a large, feathered fan. His bulky, sweating body could not reach it, a henchman placed it in his hands. He motioned for Patience to come closer. He brushed her with the feathers as she lay face down on the ground, terrified to move. She inhaled the red earth beneath her, her life flashed before her — she had plans to be a social worker, to move to Australia with Grace and Varuna; here she was, captive in a kraal at the mercy of an aging chief, his men, and complicit wives.

Patience knew Varuna's fighting spirit would not rest until she was found. Elsie chose her name as a reminder of how she expected her daughter to handle challenges she would face as a woman from a tribe that subjugated women into service and silence.

44

8

A Mother's Heart

Grace returned to Pietermaritzburg with her mother, to tap into 'contacts,' hoping for more leads to assist with Patience's return.

Hope rested with Petros Sibaya assuming a vigilante role. Varuna and Grace promised to do whatever it took, selling the wood yard or selling their home, to have Patience found.

Petros had grave reservations about being a voyeur into the chief's life; he feared this would place Grace and Varuna at risk.

'Ma V, the chief may be old but his men are blood thirsty, I will help you find Patience but fear that if I am found out, it will lead those horrible men right to you and Grace. We don't know if they have taken her or if there is another syndicate that's abducting women. I will do my best, I promise to keep you both from harm.'

'Ma V' was the familiar, respectful address from workers

at the wood yard, it was their endearing way of appreciating Varuna's good treatment of them.

'It's a blessing having you on our side. I can't count on anyone else to help us, even though I have nephews in the police force. I appreciate any help you can offer, but you must ensure your own safety at all times. Please promise me you will proceed with caution.'

'Ma V, I give you my word to do my best and leave the rest to my ancestors and the Almighty.'

He left to spend a few days gathering information on the chief's community.

*   *   *

They were aware they had to be careful if the chief had plans to make Patience his unwilling concubine. Time was running out for Grace's final completion of her studies, her demanding academic schedule forced her to return to Durban. She would keep in close contact with her mother to keep abreast with the latest on the hunt for Patience.

The adoption papers confirmed that Patience was indeed a Sharvin.

'I still can't believe you kept this a secret. The papers were signed ten years ago!'

'I didn't want to add to the burden Patience was already carrying with Elsie's illness and death, I thought it would pressurise her to relinquish her culture if I told her I was now her legal parent. Do you get what I mean? I wanted her to respect her mother's memory even though she is my dear daughter and your sister.'

'Oh mum, you always think things through to such perfection. I do understand. I know you always put the feelings and needs of others before your own.'

'Your father supported me in helping others so we were a force to be reckoned with! She smiled.

'I hope Patience is not struggling wherever she is, I know she is alive, I feel sure about this.'

'That's the way, we must remain optimistic.'

Grace returned to Durban after stacking up the cupboards and refrigerator with groceries to ensure her mother had no reason to leave the house during the week.

Petros called on Thursday afternoon with some news,

'Ma V, one of the lady's in the village said her sister, who is one of the chief's wives, told her a young woman was brought to the chief's main kraal last week. I asked her to gather more information. She needs some money to pay for her grandchild's operation. Can I offer her any money? If so how much?'

'Whatever it takes to get the information, we need confirmation that the person is Patience before I can go back to the police.'

'Are you sure Ma V?'

'Yes, please, I just want my child back...'

This was the first time she let her emotions get the better of her, she was beginning to slip up about her legal relationship with Patience.

'I know you love Patience as you did her mother, I will proceed then.'

'Where are you calling from?'

'A cell phone with a once off number, I will call you from different numbers to ensure you are not harmed Ma V.'

'Thank you, I appreciate everything you are doing for us.' He hung up.

She contemplated calling Grace with the news and decided against it as she had no tangible confirmation and did not want to raise Grace's hopes.

She pondered, fearful that Patience might not want to return to her. Perhaps she needed to reconnect with her cultural roots. Her emotions were a brewing tidal wave during her days of pensive solitude — waiting, anticipating the best and dreading the worst. She had to prepare herself for any possibility.

She pulled out a box of old videos, selecting the one marked, *Patience's Thirteenth birthday* and watched it through a river of tears. The colour and sound made the scenes in her backyard appear ancient and alien. She heard her husband's voice behind his video camera, a proud possession, he purchased in Singapore. He enjoyed videoing significant, celebrated family moments. His comment to Patience as the video ended, summed up the essence of her spirit, *Stop giggling, and give me a big smile, say something that will make you laugh when you look back at this when you are old and grey.* Varuna hung onto those final words.

The sun streamed in, waking her up to the whirring of the video machine. She watched most of the videos her husband had labelled and packed in the box. Both girls were loved with equal devotion, she wanted them to have more years together, to make new memories. This thought triggered another flood of tears.

She stood up, her knees buckled with the first signs of arthritis taking its grip. A cup of coffee was what she needed to shake her melancholia. Grace called as Varuna settled down to her morning coffee.

'Mum, how are you coping being at the house alone? Any news? Dare I ask?'

'I didn't get much sleep but I'm okay, I guess. No, don't ask. We'll chat tomorrow evening when you get in. Did you miss much on your days off from college?'

'Not too bad, I'm catching up on what I missed. My mates want to know why I cut class, something I never do. I feel awful lying that we were both unwell.'

'Yeah, I can understand, but we are both emotionally unwell so don't fret about the little white lie. It's a delicate situation as we're still in the dark, Patience's safety is paramount to us.'

'Absolutely! I'm heading to the hospital this morning for the start of my internship. Professor Irvine says I'm lucky to get a block so soon.'

'It's a good professor and place that knows a good female doctor when they meet one. I'm so proud of you Grace! Your father would have enjoyed hearing this news.'

Grace was silent on the other end. In a barely audible voice, she said, 'I know mum, I have to run. I'll call you tonight to let you know when the block begins.'

'All the best darling.' She turned off the phone and sat staring into space when the telephone rang again.

The caller was silent.

'Hello, is someone there? Grace is that you? I can't hear you.'

The line clicked, and was dead.

She dismissed it as a crossed line or rude caller who should have apologised for ringing the wrong number.

She called Anton Wessels, who she employed when a position became vacant after a long standing employee retired. Anton took a load off her in assisting with managing the wood yard.

'Hi Anton, its Varuna. How are things in the yard?'

'All going well madam. Are you unwell, you sound like you have a cold?'

'Yes, I am a little unwell. I planned to come to work this week, but it's not possible, just yet anyway. Please call me if you need anything. Are deliveries on schedule? Are the trucks in good nick? There were some burst tyre incidents last week? We must ensure the vehicles are in prime condition.'

'Don't worry at all, everything is okay, nothing untoward to report, I'll call you if need be. You should rest madam. I've not seen Petros for quite a few days. It's not like him to stay away without an explanation. Have you had news from him?'

Varuna was silent, knowing she could not reveal what Petros was up to. She explained that she sent him on an errand to Newcastle. She thanked Anton and told him not to worry, Petros would be in touch soon. She knew Anton was a well-mannered, honest man. She did not detect a trace of racism in his manner which typified some of his people. She knew he was *sweet* on Grace who would not give him the time of day. Patience often teased Grace when Anton stopped by at the house to pick up a cheque or letter from Varuna. She never failed to say, 'come on Grace, the new South Africa is approaching, it's up to you to *whiten* us a bit!' Grace would chase her around the house, throwing cushions at her as her mother watched on with joy. Grace and Patience made her home a warm and loving place. She picked up a book to distract the pervasive thoughts of her aching heart.

9

Confined

The nights were cold and draughty. The huts had no doors, a low open entrance admitted the night wind and an occasional field mouse looking for warmth and food.

Patience was placed with the chief's eldest wife, a stern old woman who did not engage in conversation unless she had to convey a message from the chief and his men.

'I hope you are fertile, the chief needs a son; he is getting old and has waited through thirteen wives and still does not have a male heir.'

Patience was silent. She wanted to voice her say on this forceful, antiquated arrangement. This was not her vision for her future. Afraid to be ridiculed because she spoke with her mother's soft, lilting tones, she remained silent.

'What do you have to say, girl? Are you barren? If you are,

you will have a very difficult time here. You will become the chief's slave.'

She listened to the hypocrisy of those words, and could not still her tongue any longer.

'Mama, you are already a slave and have been one for many years. When have you ever been out of this compound?'

'Hah! What are you saying, girl? You speak like a bewitched one. The witch doctor will beat the devil out of you!'

'Its common sense, I don't mean any disrespect, Mama. How many children do you have?'

'I have four daughters, much older than you, they are here too as the wives of the chief. As soon as they reached puberty he claimed them. I am lucky and blessed that my daughters have been chosen.'

'*That's incest, Mama!* How could you allow it? Has the chief claimed all his wives' daughters as his wives?'

'No, only fertile virgins, they had to have a child first then he gives them the privilege of moving into his quarters. My girls live like queens. They were pure, their reeds did not snap.'

Patience felt ill listening to the mother's barbaric values for her daughters and was astounded that after thirteen wives, none of his offspring would take on the baton of chieftain-ship — they were female. She realised she had to stop saying what she thought and believed. Her world had changed with the values her parents espoused, and Varuna had had a big impact on her life.

The eldest wife became a slave from the onset of puberty. Nobody questioned this cultural practice.

'The witch doctor will heal your mind and stop the nonsense you believe. You better hope she is in a good mood.'

'The witch doctor is a *woman?*' Grace was baffled that a woman had a revered position in the tribe.

'Yes, an elder who is a strong, wise woman, one who respects the chief.'

Patience felt the 'buts' ready to roll off her tongue, for now, it was best to be seen and not heard.

*   *   *

The morning of the initiation ceremony dawned, it was cold and frosty with the promise of intense rising heat at midday.

She received a ceremonial mud cleansing.

A short red skirt covered her upper thighs, multi-layered strings with multi-coloured beads were placed around her neck; they flowed onto her bare breasts. Her mother told her about the 'coming of age' initiation — this was very different — more a revenge of the older wives on the latest recruit to the chief's harem. Sitting in the scorching midday heat, mud hardened and cracked on her body. From midnight to five the next morning, she sat outside the hut staring out at the horizon, forced to contemplate her sins.

Patience willed herself to engage in mental conversations with Grace. She believed in their psychic connection. There were many times in their years growing up together when they felt the distress of each other.

*Grace you have to come and get me out of here. I don't want to end up like the eldest wife's daughters. My mother would not allow this if she was alive today. Dear God, I need to be back with **my** family.*

Patience fought the depression taking hold of her. She knew she had to entertain happy thoughts to remain clear-headed.

The witch doctor was a decrepit woman. Her small frame of protruding bones was bent like a rusty hook. Her voice was shrill. She had the strength of ten robust men.

She slapped Patience across the face, chanted in many tongues. She threw a tin of bones on the ground, gasped, her eyes rolled in dismay. Patience yelped as she pulled and tugged at her hair, as if intending to scalp her. Two of the older wives arrived, covered in brown cloaks, each holding a large, six foot, reed broom. They brushed Patience's body with its thorny vines until she bled from the rips on her skin. She forced herself to remember every detail of this live act to recount to Grace and Varuna. A younger woman stood, silently observing her, tears flooding her eyes as she performed her duties. She looked tormented with each command she received.

Patience had not braced herself for what happened next.

Her face was slit across both cheeks with a small pen knife, she felt weak as her stomach nose-dived — she slumped over into a pool of blackness.

Tribal scarification claimed her as a member of the chief's clan. Her mother told her that her father had refused to put her through this, which led to him being ostracised from the community.

*   *   *

She felt a soft caressing on her face, her eyes, swollen from the brutal cuts made it difficult to see who her gentle carer was. She heard a small, tearful voice say,

'*Eish…* I'm so sorry, I'm so sorry…'

Her throat was brittle, ready to crack, she asked for a sip of water when she tasted blood on her tongue.

Her eyes cleared as the floating image of the young woman came into view. Then her body convulsed as the rough cloth bruised her gaping facial incisions. The young woman rushed off to call the older wives.

They poured an acidic drink down her throat. She remembered the smell from her early childhood days in the village – it was the distinct smell of home-brewed beer. She balked and turned her face away when forced to take another sip. The young woman brought her a drink of water. Patience touched her hand in acknowledgement.

She knew if she had any hope of getting out of this place, it would be through the help of this young woman. She would have to rescue the young woman from this uncensored, cultural madness.

*   *   *

The next morning the swelling had subsided around her eyes. A bucket of cold water for cleaning herself, before an inspection by the wives, was placed on the floor beside her. The young woman's fear was visible — she would not make eye contact with Patience; she kept her head and body bent in servile stance.

Patience whispered, 'where is this place?'

The young woman remained silent. Patience detected a slight shaking of her head.

'Nobody can hear you, the women are too busy gossiping and drinking beer.'

'Zululand'

'How long have you been here?'

The young woman held up four fingers.

'Four years? How old were you when you arrived here?'

The eldest wife marched out towards them.

'Hurry girl, we don't have all day! You have always been too slow, that's why you are not living a queen's life like my daughters!' Her shrill, cascading guffaw thrust a squadron of starlings into the air, startled, ready to attack.

Patience's dislike of the old wife grew in intensity.

'She's out of earshot now, tell me a little about yourself.' Grace had mastered the art of speaking through unmoving lips.

The young woman looked up at the hut, bent over and whispered.

'I am from Johannesburg, my mother is Xhosa and my father is Zulu. The farm where he worked was not doing too well, so when the chief offered him a few cows as a barter for me, he agreed. My father sold me like cattle. I have not heard from my family again.' She trembled fighting back tears.

Patience felt the horror of her words – she had the urge to hug her. She thought of Goodwin Mkhize, a good father who lost his life in sparing her from such a fate, here she was now, close to being condemned to a life of servitude.

'We must get out of here, we can do this together, but cannot be seen talking to each other. Some sort of sign language is necessary.'

'It's too dangerous, the wives watch us all the time, I'm too afraid I will get caught if I tried to escape.'

'I do not want to be the chief's concubine; I prefer to die than be that – it's not the life intended for us. If you have something to warn me about when we are in group gatherings, bend over and touch your ankle or grass so I know you need to warn me about something. Can you do that?'

'I don't know, soon they will know it's a sign… I don't know.'

'Let's try it once, at least. Will you do it, please, just once?'

Patience knew this fragile soul was capable of selling her out. She had experienced much hardship that had made her a cowering, submissive woman with little sense of what was right or wrong.

The young woman agreed to try this once, she left to complete her other duties for the day.

Patience watched her walk away – she was the living dead.

10

A Helping Hand

Days became weeks, then two months, with no news if Patience would return.

Petros was inside the chief's compound after signing up as a new recruit in the role of henchman.

Varuna cautioned him to be careful as he was her only hope, the only connection to Patience.

Anton Wessels grew restless not knowing what had happened to Petros. He wanted to open a missing person's file with the local police. She knew it was time to let him know what had transpired in their lives. The truth had to be told, she had no reason to distrust him. Her intention was to keep the matter quiet for as long as possible to protect Patience from harm.

Anton arrived at three o' clock on Saturday afternoon, after shutting the wood yard for the weekend. He was a tall, golden-haired man in in his early thirties. His fringe concealed his striking blue eyes. Grace refused to sit in conversation with him, but her mother insisted it was a family matter, she needed to be present as proof of their solidarity.

'Hello madam, how are you?'

'I am well thank you, please come in.'

Anton's awkwardness was visible when he saw Grace sitting in the lounge room. His face and tips of his ears were bright red.

'Oh… nice to see you Grace. It's been a long time. How's your studying going?'

She disliked hearing the hard 'r' sound of his strong Afrikaans accent added to her name. She associated the harshness with the vernacular her father's sisters' spoke whenever she was within ear-shot of their conversations about her mother. She noticed Anton's downy haired arms and legs. The outdoor work he did at the wood yard had tanned his skin to a reddish-brown hue, unlike his pale head of hair. He wore a khaki shirt and shorts. Grace squirmed when she saw his knee high green socks and brown boots. She had an aversion to game park ranger uniforms and they reminded her of the attire of the Afrikaner *AWB* movement, the Afrikaner neo-Nazi separatist political organisation. Her mother refused to accept Grace's perception of Anton, she expected nothing else but politeness when invited guests were in their home.

'Hello Anton. Nice to see you too. Studying is hectic now.'

'Soon we will have a doctor in the family.' Varuna beamed with pride, much to Grace's embarrassment.

'Wonderful, all the best hey, *ja* you've done well, you must be so proud, madam.'

'Thank you, Anton, would you like a cup of tea or coffee?' As a quick exit before Varuna made any further comments, Grace suggested tea or coffee as an appealing diversion.

'No, nothing for me thanks. *Ja*, madam I made sure I got here today because I'm worried about Petros. You know the nature of crime here and it disturbs me, he has been away with no contact.'

'Anton, I need your absolute trust.'

He darted a look in Grace's direction, he sat upright in his seat.

'What is it madam, is he in trouble?'

Varuna told him about Patience's abduction and the fear they had.

'Ag, shame. This is not good at all. I did not know. I apologise for badgering you so much about Petros' whereabouts. Has he gone looking for her then? I can only imagine how stressed you are.'

Grace softened a little when she heard his genuine concern.

'Yes Anton, we cannot say anything to jeopardise her safety.'

'What can I do?' He wanted to help them with genuine, pleading concern. Varuna was the first employer who treated him with respect, listening to him, accepting his opinions.

'When I have word from Petros, I will let you know. If you need assistance at the wood yard, I could recall Amos from retirement.'

'No, no, I'm coping madam. I was just worried, you know. It's better not to have too many people asking questions, although Amos is a hell of a nice bloke. Please know you can trust me, madam.'

'I do, thank you. For the moment, we have to keep a low profile as the police have shoved us aside, saying they don't get involved in cultural matters. This is a criminal act, but they are adamant. This is why so many are killed with no consequences for the perpetrators. I am really tired of the apathy in this country.'

'My brother-in-law is a cop, madam, in Klipriver, I could ask him if he could put pressure here to help us. He's a big boy there, he has a lot of influence; you know what I mean.'

'I need to mull over this before we approach the police again.

Additional problems have to be avoided while Petros is in the chief's den.'

'Okay, I understand, madam, please call me anytime. You and Grace should be careful as you move around town. How you feel about getting a bodyguard to watch over you?'

Grace jumped in, 'No, that will draw attention to us, my mother is not leaving the house unless there is an emergency. I leave after sunset on a Sunday so that gives me some protection from public glare.'

'I won't insist but think of it as an option. I am not volunteering myself but there are people who are available if I ask.'

They thanked him for his support and concern and advised him to be careful should shysters approach him.

Anton left, unsettled.

'We are fortunate to have Anton, he is loyal but can be too trusting at times. I have not told you yet, I had an odd telephone call, a silent caller this week. It could have been a wrong number but the person hung on, listening to my voice or whatever else they hoped to hear. I'm not letting it unravel me.'

'Mum, knowing your family, it could well be a nosy-parker wanting to know what you are up to. News must be flying around that you are not in the wood yard these days, small town folk talk.'

'You might be right Grace, ever since your father passed on, they have criticised everything I do; they have nothing else to do! Varuna felt immense pressure but was mindful not to neglect Grace's needs.

'Tell me about your internship, have you been enjoying it?'

'Its hard work but an amazing experience which confirms dad's dream of me being a doctor. I love it and feel so humbled when patients look at me with such respect and hope. It's a huge responsibility.'

'That makes me happy, but don't devote your whole life to your job. It will be good to have grandchildren from you and Patience while I have the strength and energy!'

She felt relieved seeing her mother relax.

A loud banging on the front door and an urgent booming voice disturbed them,

'Madam are you in there? Open the door please!'

Grace opened the security gate to two police officers, peering in; their eyes searching behind her with an invasive, sinister air.

Her heart skipped a beat — was there news, had something happened to Patience?

'Where is Mrs. Sharvin? She has to come to the station to make a statement.'

'What's up officer, what statement is she required to make?'

'Just call your mother, I presume, or we will take her to the station ourselves.'

Varuna heard the commotion, she walked towards Grace,

'What seems to be the matter?'

'These police officers require a statement from you down at the station for some reason.'

'What is this about sir?'

'You laid a complaint about a missing person, we have a counter report suggesting you have had the individual abducted so we need a formal statement to confirm your stand. You can come ride in our vehicle or follow us to the station.'

'Thank you, I will ride over on my own! Who made such a ridiculous accusation?'

'That will be detailed at the station.'

'Please give me five minutes to lock up the house. How long will this take officer?'

'As long as you make it, madam.'

Grace appealed to her mother to think before she blurted out anything that could incriminate her in this bizarre situation.

They entered the police station with heightening dread.

'Mrs. Sharvin, this does not involve your daughter, would you like her to leave the room?'

'No sir, unless she chooses to.'

'Miss Sharvin do you wish to leave the room while we question your mother?'

'I wish to remain to support my mother.'

'Fill out all documentation laid out before you to verify your presence and response to the allegation.'

'We want to know what documents you expect my mother to verify. We require more information on the accusation before any incriminating documents are signed.'

'Ahem! Mrs. Sharvin, again, I ask, are you happy with her being a self-elected spokesperson for you? Are you not capable of stating your own reservations?'

'She will ask whatever questions she wants, in my interest, I'm no doubt stressed and concerned about this, I don't know why I've been hauled in as if I am the criminal.'

'*Criminal?* Nobody has said you were, yet, anyway?'

Varuna shot Grace an anxious look, terrified that some sinister scam was afoot.

'The reason is that we have a charge laid against you, alleging you abducted Patience Sharvin. It's a protocol that we have to act upon this allegation. The records show you adopted her a few years ago.'

'Who has made this charge against me?' Varuna's usual calm demeanour gradually ebbed as she insisted on knowing who her enemy was.

'Before I provide this answer, how do you respond? I have to record everything you say. You will be shown the report before you append your signature to it.'

'It's bizarre, how can I be guilty when I'm grieving over my daughter's disappearance? I did not abduct Patience.' Varuna's frayed nerves were obvious, her tremulous voice and struggle to hold back tears were ignored.

'I have no reason to have her abducted, I am living out my promise to her dead, biological mother.'

'The concern is that you disappeared in Johannesburg with her. You laid a missing person charge in Johannesburg. We also have on record that Patience Sharvin was required to return to the chief's domicile, back to her tribal community. You refused this command. Am I correct?'

'Yes, I could not send her to strangers. Which parent would do such a thing? I promised her mother she would not be forced to marry. We left for Johannesburg to keep her safe.'

Varuna let out an uncontrolled sob. Grace looked at her unsure how to calm her in this awful vendetta.

'Mrs. Sharvin, there appears reason you could have staged the kidnapping or abduction of Patience to avoid the tribal intervention. We have to take the charge against you as legitimate, we believe you have reason to have done this.'

Grace stood up, her chest puffed out, head held high and announced, 'my mother needs representation; this sounds far more serious than someone creating mischief. We cannot say anything further until our family lawyer has been solicited and briefed. May we leave?'

'Your legal representation might make this *very* messy, just tell us where you have hidden Miss Patience?'

'I have not hidden her anywhere!' Varuna raised her voice, losing all sense of equanimity under the emotional weight of the accusation.

Grace cut in, 'may we leave officer as we have no legal representation, and I will hold you liable if my mother collapses under the strain you are putting her under.'

'*Really?* That's a *huge* claim. You may leave, but remember you are being watched, *both* of you are!'

Grace put her arm around her mother to steady her. As they walked out onto the corridor, she heard the questioning officer say, 'bloody upstart, who does she think she is? These people make me sick, they get a bit of education and think they can lay down the law! I hate to think what this country is going to be like when these people take over!'

The day started out with the promise of a resolution in the offing to Patience being found.

Now they were suspects in an uncanny twist of events.

11

Tears of Hope

I t was the dreaded night of her purity test, the reed dance held her fate – if she was a virgin, she would have the highest status as the latest concubine in the chief's harem.

*   *   *

Patience washed and dressed under the watchful eyes of the older wives. She looked at herself in the mirror for the first time since her arrival. Her heart lurched when she saw the deep incisions on her cheeks, two on each cheek. The older wives ululated, bleating like sheep out of rhythm when they saw her studying her scars.

'Now you are beautiful and ready to see the chief,' the eldest wife said.

'I hope for your sake the reed does not bend nor crack,' she mocked, narrowing her eyes with a sinister air of superiority.

'Well, I have nothing to fear, I am untouched if that's what you mean.'

A chorus of hyena laughter erupted from the wives, they threw back their heads, stamped their feet, raising red dust as they revelled in Patience's discomfort on the fate that awaited her.

The young woman assured Patience, with calm certainty, she would not be the next concubine. She said the older wives had manipulative, private agendas.

They arrived at the chief's compound. He sat on his throne, head lowered to his chest, in a deep sleep.

A warm breeze caressed Patience's skin. The torches were lit, elongated, hazy shadows were cast on the red earth. She sat in the front row of the group of forty women — their purity was up for public scrutiny. Her reed was thick, firm, and a tad green. Waves of nausea took hold as butterflies did a convulsive dance in her belly – her possible future husband sat on his wooden throne; he was old enough to be her great-grandfather. *How could she live with such a man as his wife? How was she to bear his children?* Repulsion infused her being — all she wanted was to die in that moment. She looked up at the henchmen behind the chief. She squinted in the torchlight – to the right, four men down the line, stood a familiar figure!

Patience squinted again, straining her eyes — goose bumps rose from her ankles to her skull — it was Petros! She wanted to shout out to him, questions exploded in her brain. *How could he betray her, Varuna and Grace this way? Did he have her abducted in Johannesburg?* She stared at him, aware he was looking right at her! Her head ached, her knees wobbled as waves of gasps rose into the night air. She felt herself being lifted to her feet, the reed was placed in her hands again. Somebody wound her fingers around the stick to keep it fixed in her grasp.

The first henchman, to the left of the chief, propped the chief's head up, off his chest, for a view of his next concubine, his ear lobes were stretched down to his shoulders with decades of wearing large, disk-shaped wooden earrings. She prayed her reed would snap, it felt thinner and drier than the one she held earlier. Her mind drummed over and over again, *snap, snap, snap!*

The young woman attempted to conceal her faint smile. This was her doing, the reed had been swapped when she fainted. She stood paralysed, waiting for her verdict. She walked to the back of the line aware that the young woman was doubled over in a fit of giggles. Through clenched teeth, Patience said, 'you changed the reed! It was thin and dry, why did it not snap?'

'Wait, please no questions, I have a plan.' The young woman spoke with new confidence and certainty, seducing Patience with the hope she was offering. Her thoughts flitted back to Petros. As a teenager, she admired his lithe body which reminded her of the San people. She knew if he was involved in her kidnapping, she was doomed to remain there for the rest of her days. He knew everything about her and the Sharvin family.

Late that night, a violent storm shook the compound – red earth now thick bloody pools of stagnant water, smaller huts and trees lay collapsed in a mangled mess, sending whispers of the devil unleashing his wrath.

*　　*　　*

The chief was ill. He was too weak to fight tuberculosis that had ravaged his breathing in recent months.

Patience and the young woman waited in the women's quarters for word when she would be required to fulfil her wifely obligations — news came to them like a rainbow after a savage storm that a slaughtering ritual, to appease the ancestors, was being prepared. This sacrificial feast would restore the chief's health. His wellbeing was paramount until the birth of a male child to seal the tribe's future.

On the night of the feast, the community gathered in the arena to pray. The chief's henchmen were in the forefront, the wives stood in the background after preparing meat, potatoes, corn, and beer.

The young woman looked forward to a substantial meal. It was a buffet, an *all you could eat without being watched feast.*

Patience caught a glimpse of Petros attempting to make eye contact with her. She did not want to talk to him for fear she would be punished.

The young woman served the chief's henchmen while the older wives attended to the ill chief.

The first offering was for the men. Their consumption of the carcass was a ritual, believed to have the potency to restore male health.

Petros reached out for the meat. He placed a tiny rolled paper under the tray. Patience noticed his closed eyes and moving lips as one who was praying.

The young woman appeared unsettled. Patience wondered if he was coercing the unassuming young woman into making things difficult for her. The young woman returned with the empty wooden tray, brushed up against Patience and stuck the tiny rolled paper in the waist band of her grass skirt.

After two hours of feasting, the women departed to their quarters. Patience reached into her waist band.

The paper was not there.

'I seem to have dropped the paper you placed in my waistband.'

'I must go back to the exact spot where we stood.'

'It will be impossible to find if the torches are out. The night sky is an impenetrable black, no moon, no stars in sight. Perhaps you can go out at sunrise.'

'And risk being caught *and* killed? The same fate will await you.'

'I saw the henchman talking to you. What did he say?'

'He told me to give you the paper; that is all.'

'Without the note, we do not know what he wants.'

The young woman disappeared into the inky night. Her heightened animal instincts and familiarity with the terrain made her a determined hunter rather than a victim.

She returned an hour later with a dusty scrap of paper.

They feared to strike a match to light a candle. The older wives were on watch. Sunrise was a safer option.

Neither Patience nor the young woman slept a wink that night. At the rising of the sun, they studied the dusty, rolled note, holding it up to catch the light.

A faint scrawl read:

I am here to take you home. Watch me, never taking your eyes off me.

Patience was not one for an excessive show of vulnerability, now she sobbed with relief. The surprised young woman whispered, 'be happy, not sad. There's hope for you leaving this god-forsaken place, wash away your sadness.'

'I'm crying tears of happiness, I have hope, and tears of unhappiness for mistrusting the reason Petros is here. I will not leave without you, that's a promise.'

The young woman smiled, her years of subjugation had hardened her belief that freedom was possible for her.

'If trying to take me with you, creates problems as it will, you should leave without me. I have learned to live with this situation. Before you depart, I have one question, Petros is quite a handsome man. Is he married?'

Patience smiled, happy that a youthful spark was still alive in the young woman's vacuous world.

'No, he's not married. Let's see what happens, I plan to take you with me, out of this hell-hole.'

12

News

Grace buried herself in studying. She trusted that Petros would deliver on his promise to bring Patience back to them.

The paperwork for their application to the Australian High Commission was almost complete. The final steps were medical and police clearance requirements. Extended weekend working hours at the pharmacy helped to grow the nest egg needed to settle in Australia. More hours at the hospital would add to her professional experience, necessary to secure a good position overseas.

Two months passed with no news from Patience.

Grace and Varuna continued to live secluded from social contact. The police dropped the charges of abduction against Varuna as a hoax, with no further explanations. No follow-up consideration for the stress created, confirmed the necessity of the move to Australia. Varuna never got over the false charge and repetitively speculated on who could have been responsible for putting her through the horrible trauma.

'I'm still pondering over who did this and what could have been the motivation for it?'

'Let it go mum, we can guess who did it. Years of jealousy and petty family politics almost ended your marriage to dad, but God bless his soul, for not allowing wagging tongues to destroy the love you shared.'

'It saddens me that family cannot see their own, happy or prospering. It's a blessing that Elsie and Patience came into our lives. Patience will be back soon, the next chapter of our lives is already written.'

'That promise keeps me getting up each day.'

'How are things at the hospital?'

'Don't get me started on that, sexism is rife and being an Indian woman does not make my life any easier. Dr. Raja's rudeness is incomprehensible. Dad treated you with respect, he did not pigeonhole women, but Dr. Raja is a piece of work! He drops crass comments that a woman's place is in the kitchen or on her back! Can you believe his audacity?'

'Oh yes, I can, the mongrel! He is a typical old school idiot! Which planet does he live on? I wish I could give him a piece of my mind.'

'No way, mum! It's under control. The least said the better. He will get a rude awakening one day at the hands of his own daughters. I heard through the hospital grapevine, he has two daughters in primary school.'

'Yes leave it to the law of karma. You should say something to assert yourself though, Grace, maybe he will stop if you do.'

'I think it will make him more aggressive, my silence keeps him guessing whether I will report him to HR.'

'Good thinking. Every challenge in life is destined to make you a better person.'

'It really doesn't feel that way when you face this every day. I don't want to think about the toad! We should begin clearing out household goods to prepare for our big move. This creates positive energy, we can keep essentials and throw out the rest. I don't suggest tackling Patience's room though.'

Grace added in the last comment, knowing from experience her mother's frenzied cleaning mode resulted in valuable goods being turned over to those in need with no thought for their needs!

'I will start with the kitchen, we should do this piecemeal to avoid drawing attention to ourselves.'

'That's a good way to start. While I am away during the week, you can get started on the kitchen and I will work on my room when I'm home during weekends.' Grace had to spell out what needed to be done, her mother was cracking under the emotional strain of Patience's abduction, constantly playing out things in her mind. Suspending her usual activities made her absent-minded, leaving her confused about the day of the week or the time of day.

The doorbell rang – they were not expecting anyone. Footsteps were heard running off — the camera didn't capture the doorbell ringer – the recording device was turned off.

'Mum, why do you turn the recorder off, we need constant surveillance more so than ever now!'

'I relax a little when you are home, Grace, I make sure it's turned on when you're away.'

'Please mum, this is not a time to be reckless about safety. It has to be recording, twenty-four seven!'

'I miss the old days when doors were not locked, there was nothing to fear, now we lock everything including locking ourselves away. How times have changed,' she sighed.

'We need to adapt as women on our own. Crime against women is the worst in the world. We must proceed with caution to avoid becoming another forgotten statistic.'

'One of us better get that door; it's pointless arguing.'

Grace went to the front door, Varuna turned on the surveillance monitor. A white envelope jutted from under the doormat, Grace picked it up.

'It's a letter with your name on the envelope, it seems to be hand delivered – no postage stamp.'

'That looks like Petros' handwriting.' Varuna ripped the envelope open, eager for news on Patience. She read the note to Grace.

All is OK. It might be a few weeks more before we are home. Do not worry.

'Seems he cannot include any details lest the note reaches unintended hands, the capitalised 'OK' is comforting.'

'It's nerve wracking having to wait and not having a direct word from Patience. It's killing me Grace!'

They hugged each other, two lonely souls, hanging onto hope in a senseless world. Varuna suggested a cup of tea as her cure for all ills.

'Tea? I need a gin and tonic.'

'Grace, you said our safety is paramount, how will you be alert after a gin and tonic?' Varuna's wittiness was the lightening tonic needed.

'Your sense of humour, makes Patience seem more your daughter than I am.'

'I miss her laughter ringing through the house, I hope she's...'

The telephone rang as they sipped a refreshing cup of *Rooibos* tea.

'Hello, Varuna speaking.'

'Madam. Anton here. I have something to tell you ...'

Varuna cut him off before he could finish his sentence.

'Can you come over Anton?'

He realised Varuna was being cautious about talking on the telephone.

'Yes, I could be there in an hour, is that suitable?'

'Yes Anton, come over for tea, I'll rustle up a batch of crumpets.'

Grace scowled at her mother for inviting Anton to tea.

'He has something to tell us, I could not let him say whatever it was on the telephone. Please be hospitable when he comes over. Smile.'

'I'm always hospitable, I'm your daughter, remember?'

*   *   *

Anton arrived, concerned, wanting to unburden his troubles.

'Is something the matter at the wood yard Anton?'

'No madam, oh hello Grace. Sorry, I don't mean to disturb you. A note's arrived from Petros. I found it on my desk at work. He must have put it there, its hand delivered. Here it is.'

'Thank you for coming over Anton, Grace and I received a letter too, it does not say much but offers hope that Patience might be unharmed.'

'Is it from Petros, madam?'

'Yes, it appears to be his handwriting.'

'Are you both okay, Grace? I've been worried about your safety ever since my last visit.'

'We are frustrated that we have no control in this situation, waiting is making us nervous.'

Varuna read out the note to Grace.

Baas, things are not good, I will not be back to work for a while. Keep the family safe. The main man is ill. I will reunite all soon.

'I appreciate that he does not mention names but your letter is a little unsettling if he says 'things are not good.' I assume 'the main man' is the chief so that is a little comforting that the chief's illness is providing a level of protection for Patience. What do you think Anton?'

'Petros is concerned about your wellbeing. I wondered why he called me 'baas' so unlike him, that is why I thought it was someone posing as him in the note.'

'He is protecting you, should the letter go astray; he knew we would decipher the message.'

'Did you speak to anyone from the tribe to find out more? I wish I knew who delivered the note.'

'No, I've been house bound. Grace has cautioned me to avoid speaking to anyone. You could check the office surveillance backup if you want to find out who delivered the note.'

'With your permission, I will. May I try to find out what's going on with the chief? Petros can offer limited communication from inside. If I can find the person who delivered the note, this might be a way forward.'

Varuna looked at Grace for confirmation. Grace took this as her cue to say something.

'That might bring us more news, however, we do not want to complicate your life too.'

'I'm happy to assist, and the offer to get my brother-in-law involved through police intervention still stands.'

'Thank you, Anton, perhaps when there's more information to go on.'

'I will only do as you ask. Is there anything else I can do to assist today?'

Grace had to humble herself to ask, 'Anton, as I'm away during the week if my mother needs medical attention, may she call you to assist her with whatever she needs. It would take an hour for me to get to her.'

Varuna felt embarrassed that 'care' was being arranged for her.

'Grace, I'm not an invalid, I should be fine.' She was indignant that her distress and odd spells of dizziness were being construed as perhaps needing medical care.

'I won't trouble you, madam, only if you ask, I promise.' Anton smiled knowing Grace was being the protective daughter. He admired her all the more for this.

He left the note with Varuna, accepted the wrapped crumpets with a thankful smile and a quick last glance at Grace before slipping out the door.

13

The Hand of Fate

A loud, mournful wailing erupted from the chief's kraal at six o'clock that morning. This brought everyone out of their huts rushing up the hill to investigate the commotion.

Petros slipped out of sight. He immersed himself in the throngs of people milling around the chief's compound as he made his way to Patience's hut. Distraction and chaos was a godsend for an unnoticed getaway. He peered in at the window. There was no sign of Patience.

The stench of cow dung reached his nostrils. Patience was under instruction to resurface the yard of the women's quarters. He was unsure if it was Patience he saw, she appeared thinner, there was a still quietness about her — her vibrant spirit appeared absent. She worked with monotonous motion, scooping, laying and flattening the cow dung to a smooth surface. She was unaware of Petros' presence behind her. He made a squawking sound mimicking the Mallard duck. Patience had become attuned to familiar rural sounds around her. Months of waiting had sharpened her senses, this sound was foreign — she turned around to see Petros with a finger to his lips, and with a flick of this head, he motioned her to approach him.

'The chief passed away during the early hours of the morning. We must get away while things are chaotic. We have to walk a long distance to where a car is ready for us to drive back to Ma V. You must listen to what I say, please Patience. I am now in equal danger as you, we must avoid being caught.'

Petros knew Patience was strong-willed and argumentative when things made her uncomfortable.

'What do you want me to do? There is another, a young woman; she must come with us.'

'*Eish*, that's not possible. It will draw attention to us, one man and two women. It's easier with two backs to watch, three becomes complicated.

'Please Petros, we must take her with us, she has protected me in here. He put his fingers to his lips to quieten her raised voice.

'It's not a good idea, sorry sister, we should get going.'

The young woman stepped out with a fresh bucket of cow dung. She stopped dead in her tracks when she saw Petros.

'This is so dangerous', she hissed, looking at them with shocked worry, 'you must leave now, the wives will whip us first and then summon the henchmen.'

'Patience and I are leaving now.'

She looked at Patience, 'the time has come, leave now!'

'You must leave with us!'

'We must go before the grief-stricken women return Patience,' Petros urged.

'You both leave, I will stall questions and a search for you to allow you to get to safety, go now!' The young woman shoved

Patience, her wide-eyed fear was for her own safety too, she would be beaten for aiding and abetting a runaway. The wives were cruel tormentors.

Petros and Patience set off on foot walking at first and then picking up to a running pace into the heat of the rolling savanna before them. The summer had begun with the ferocity of lost memory for the recent winter.

A car was available for them in Empangeni. Petros had arranged everything while he was inside the kraal. Navigating the heat and urgency to avoid drawing attention to themselves, meant they had to appear to be man and wife. Patience did not want to appear submissive, she had to obey him if she hoped to stay alive.

*   *   *

They arrived in Empangeni under cover of darkness. Patience's blistered feet slowed them down. Mama Elsie always ensured she wore sand shoes when she played outdoors, Varuna bought her comfortable shoes to match the many dresses she had.

The trek across treacherous terrain, skulking like hunted kudu in dense bushland was far removed from the life she had in the Sharvin home. Petros' insensitive remark in an unthinking moment injured her feelings, 'you take the girl from her tribe and culture is gone with the wind eh!'

'Look, Petros, thanks for what you're doing, please no jokes of that sort at a time like this.'

'Ah, sorry sister, I thought you like to laugh all the time. I'm being silly, please don't tell Ma V about this, I don't want her upset after all she's been through.'

'Now why would I tell her about your silliness when she placed so much trust in you?'

'Thank you. We shall stop at a pharmacy and motel to get you cleaned up, I can't take you back in a poor condition.'

'I'll survive, I'm not going to any motel with you!'

'I will wait outside while you get cleaned up.'

'Please take me home, I don't want to stop off anywhere.'

'We need to make a petrol stop, would you like something to eat?'

'Just water, please, I need a lot of water.'

'I'm hungry, we've been grazing on dry bread while walking, please eat something.'

'You go ahead, don't mind me, I am just anxious to get home.'

They turned on the car radio closer to Pietermaritzburg.

There has been no further news from the Chief's inside source, some quarters speculate that the funeral will take place in a week. This will bring Pietermaritzburg to a standstill. People travelling through the city are advised to seek information on restrictions and delays before entering the town centre. Preparations by the municipal council are underway. Listen in for more information in the days ahead.

'The wives must have realised by now that I have left or will they be too grief-stricken to notice my absence?'

'They will know by now.'

'The young woman we left behind will be in a great deal of trouble. Will you be able to go back for her?'

'I don't know Patience, I am now an enemy of the tribe because I left without seeking permission to do so. It is necessary for me to go into hiding for a while after this.'

'Thank you for risking everything to get me out, Petros. I might seem aloof but that is how I protect myself. Living with Mama Varuna and Grace has been a blessing but it came with a lot of criticism from my own people and others throughout my childhood, and even now as you can see.'

*   *   *

Seeing her home again as they turned into the driveway, the place of many years of love and happiness, lit her lamp of gratitude.

Varuna was an emotional wreck, wanting to laugh with joy and relief and cry for the hardship Patience endured. Petros drove into the garage to avoid snooping neighbours.

'I'm running you a bath first, your feet look sore and swollen. You must eat something, you have wasted away.'

'I would prefer a shower first and soak in the tub later. It's late, I can't eat anything now, or maybe just a slice of toast. Mama, Petros was amazing. He protected me all the way back to you and Grace.'

Patience held back her emotions, not wanting Petros to see her vulnerable side. She held onto Grace and Varuna trying to talk through her sobs.

'I believed I would die in there. The chief's illness offered temporary protection. Once he was well again, marriage and a child would be demanded. It's so good to be home again.'

Grace tried to break the awkward situation, observing Petros standing aside, looking away, his eyes bloodshot, not knowing what to say or do.

'Enough with the hugs now, we will all need to shower with the dust caked on your skin and clothes!'

Petros managed a smile.

'You should shower and eat too, Petros, you must be exhausted and hungry.'

'Ma, I think I should go home before anybody comes looking for me. I found out a lot about how the henchmen operate, from working alongside them. They will be coming for Zulu justice.'

Varuna never failed to have a warm kitchen and a full plate

of food for those who entered her home. Grace knew it was cultural practice that nobody should leave one's home without a meal or at the very least a cup of tea and a biscuit.

'Thank you Ma V, you can pack a little dinner, I'll eat it on my way home. I will be in touch. You may tell Anton what has happened. He is a good man. I cannot return to the wood yard just yet.'

'I understand, you need to protect yourself. Be safe. See you when things settle.'

*　　*　　*

Patience lay on the couch recounting the days spent at the compound in Zululand. She spoke of the older wives cruelty and their die-hard allegiance to the chief. Varuna added her understanding of why the women declared their loyalty to a situation that abused them.

'The wives enjoy a level of comfort and 'protection,' as the older 'chosen' wives. They would be fearful of returning to their villages where they were unsure about getting their next meal. I have also heard the chief was quite a generous man and mellowed in his old age.'

'Yes, I see your point, Mama, the older wives seem to run their own ship in their section of the compound, but that's not a life… the chief appeared mellow and disconnected from things. He dozed off during the feasts, which was a sign, he was ailing.'

'If you had a child with him, there was no chance you could leave. I suspect that is also why the older wives remain as they do,' Grace added.

'That thought makes me sick. I think we need to change the subject, I want family news.'

'I graduate in three months. I'm in the throes of finishing up my internship.'

'Have I been away that long?'

'The Australian High Commission is calling for our final paperwork, we are almost there. We started paring down household contents.'

'I don't know how I will cope after you've gone. It will take time to arrange my refugee papers.'

'Refugee papers?' Grace looked at Varuna. The time had come to reveal their family situation.

Patience sat still, tears brimming as she listened to every word Varuna said on her adoption. She looked at the adoption papers, wiped away her tears and said,

'I declare, my dear Grace, we are sisters after all!' All three did a little dance of joy with Patience pulling Varuna onto her feet, bumping bottoms and shoulders in a fit of giggles.

'Yes 'Patience Sharvin,' you will not be going to Australia as a refugee but as one of the Sharvin clan!'

'Grace you kept this from me all these years!'

'No dear sister, I found out the well-guarded secret from your mother here, after your abduction.'

'This calls for some champagne tonight, I have forgotten what it tastes like!'

*　　*　　*

At the breakfast table, the next morning, Grace heard the television morning show announcement that breaking news was coming up after the commercial break. They took their coffee mugs and gathered in the family room, curious if the breaking news was about the chief's death.

Last night, a violent outbreak, at the bus depot in the east end

of the city, led to three fatalities. Police are investigating the reason for this senseless gun fire that put many people's lives at risk. One of the three killed is identified as Petros Sibaya. Police are urging the public to come forward with any information that will lead to finding the men who gunned down innocent civilians. Now back to yesterday's parliament sitting...

All three sat frozen, staring at the television screen... fear crept back, deep into their souls...

They had nothing to celebrate.

14

Senseless Killing

The police turned a deaf ear to Varuna's insistence that the chief's clan engineered Petros' murder. The chief's world was still off limits to the police even after his passing — a fortress of secrecy sealed off the compound from public and media gaze.

Preparation for a new life in Australia came to a grinding halt, sadness lingered in silence.

Anton Wessels was a tower of strength. He cautioned Varuna and Grace to leave things as they were to ensure their safety.

'How can I ignore what has happened. Petros died while helping us to be a family again. How can I live in peace with such an awful memory, Anton?'

'Madam, you do not know if the chief's men shot him. It could have been a random heist, typical of this crime-ridden country. The police ditch investigations because thousands more are waiting for answers.'

'That's awful, many people like us are leaving the country. So much is vested here, years spent building a life; this is our homeland, country of our birth, yet we feel driven out in a bid to save ourselves. Who are we to turn to for justice in this troubled land?'

'I know how you feel madam, but believe me when I say nobody seems to care like you do anymore. It sounds terrible when I hear myself say this, but there's no running away from this fact. Why should you suffer under this senseless inhumanity? Find peace madam, you deserve that now.'

'Anton, you are too kind, I will worry about your safety when I'm in Australia.'

'I will be fine, thank you for trusting me to continue running the wood yard. I will visit you and I know you will come back for a visit too.'

Varuna gave Petros' a princely send-off, a grand funeral was held at the community hall in town. His tombstone read with accurate simplicity:

Here is a selfless man, taken too soon.
Petros Sibaya
1969-1999
May He Rest in Eternal Peace

*   *   *

With two months left for the final trek to Australia, they were living out of suitcases with minimum household essentials. The house was sold – a slippery real estate agent sealed off a rapid deal to an overseas investor for an undisclosed 'extra cash' hand-over of funds which was deposited into his personal Swiss bank account.

Grace had not called home for two days leaving her mother stressed that yet another daughter appeared to have slipped off the family radar. Anton offered to drive to Durban to check on her, but word arrived that she was unwell and infectious with a high fever.

Varuna's, maternal instinct told her something had disturbed her daughter, her silence and weekend away from home was out of character. Part of her hoped Grace had met a man and was not ready to introduce him to the family.

When she returned two weeks later, she was subdued and reclusive. Her reason for hiring a car was brushed aside as her car being stolen from outside her apartment.

She refused food or company.

'Are you still feeling unwell? It's not like you to sleep all day. The pharmacist called to ask if you were coming in to do your shift this weekend. He is concerned that you were not in last weekend and again this weekend. You need to speak to him.'

'I'm a little tired, please tell him I will return to work next weekend. Tell Patience I don't want to infect you both so I'm staying locked in my room. You should go back downstairs mum.'

'May I bring you some soup?'

'My appetite is non-existent, I'll be fine, I need the rest, don't worry.'

'If you say so. You do need sustenance to energise you, but you know that. Your graduation dinner is next week, you should go to Dr. Jorgens for a general check. Perhaps you are a little anaemic?'

'Rest is all I need.' She closed her eyes and turned to face the wall, shutting down her mother's concerns. Patience calmed

Varuna by saying that Grace had had a stressful few months of working long days, completing her internship, finalising the move to Australia and the emotional stress created by her disappearance. They agreed they all needed space after the treacherous past months.

*   *   *

Grace's graduation ceremony was a grand affair. Top medics in their fields, from surgeons, obstetricians, cosmetic surgeons and general practitioners delivered spectacular speeches on their chosen areas of medical science. They praised the next generation of doctors for the contributions they would make to South African health and advancement in medical research. Grace remained morose and aloof throughout the formalities. Sadness hung around Varuna, this would have been a proud moment for her husband. Seeing his daughter among respected peers of the medical profession, was what he hoped for, to see Grace make a name for herself with the opportunities he lacked in his life.

They paid their respects at his grave site earlier in the day. Grace was teary during these visits. Today she was unemotional, distant, and preoccupied.

Dr. Raja, Grace's intern supervisor, walked towards them. She stood up, walked out the room, leaving her mother and Patience red-faced and awkward, forced to converse with the insufferable man.

'That's a pity,' he said, 'I wanted to congratulate Grace tonight. Mrs. Sharvin, I hope she brings you many grandchildren in the years ahead. You need a big family now.' He ignored Patience, looking right past her towards the exit, hoping Grace would return.

'Thank you Dr. Raja; that's the furthest thought on my mind.

Grace, like Patience, is independent and career oriented. We appreciate that you stopped to offer your congratulations, we shall pass that on to Grace. Please excuse us, enjoy the evening.' They hurried outdoors to find Grace. She stood on the patio, alone in the faint drizzle that had started, lost in a reverie, unaware Patience was calling out to her.

'We met the awful Dr. Raja. Thanks for leaving us at his mercy!' Patience laughed. 'Let's go in for the delightful finger food and a glass of wine.'

'And risk bumping into that despicable man again, no thank you! I suggest we go out to the seafood restaurant at the beach.'

Varuna piped in when she realised Patience looked upset by Grace's non-negotiated change of dinner plans. 'Good idea, let's get out of here, the pomp and ceremony and rajas are stifling!' The evening was stilted as each one struggled to feel joy.

Grace switched off to the conversation about what Patience and her mother hoped for in Australia. The only time she responded was when Varuna asked her how her Skype job interview went.

'I'm glad I found a position in rural New South Wales. A country town will be a good place to start my career and our new lives. I'm expected to hold the position for two years.'

'How will we ever repay you for this golden opportunity to start over again?'

'Please Patience, no need for sentiments now. Where would I be without you two?'

'This calls for another bottle of wine.' Varuna was keen to inject some merriment into the evening.

'Not for me thanks, I'm the designated driver tonight. You both knock yourselves out.' Her blunt manner left them unsure what was the right thing to say.

'It's your night, Grace, have some fun,' Patience pleaded.

'I changed my mind about crashing at my apartment, we are going back to Pietermaritzburg after dinner.'

Varuna abandoned thoughts of ordering another bottle of wine. Grace saw the disappointment in her mother's eyes and tried to recover the moment, 'we can have a bottle when we get home and watch the sun rise.'

Varuna mentally explained away Grace's terse attitude as her grieving for her father who desired to see his daughter capped as a medic.

*   *   *

They got back to Pietermaritzburg around midnight and decided a cup of coffee was a better option if they were to see the sun rise.

'We must relish our treasured experiences here, the sunrise is beautiful.'

'I hear that the skyline in Australia and New Zealand are incomparable in their clarity and definition.'

'Well, that's something to look forward to.'

They lauded South African delicacies, and perhaps they might not eat adorable kangaroos. Patience was an adventurous eater, she would try any gustatory delight when she hit Australia. She reminded them, kangaroos only looked adorable but could kick the daylights out of them when angered.

A faint sound at the door caught their attention.

'Did you hear that sound, what is it?' Grace asked.

'Sounded like a kitten, I think. Let's look.'

'Check the surveillance monitor first Patience. I cannot believe how negligent you and mum can be with rushing to the door with no sense of security!' Grace lost her cool — her outburst silenced Patience who agreed that they had to be careful.

92

The front entrance light bulb was fused, nothing was clear on the monitor on this drizzly night.

All three tip-toed to the door. Grace took the lead, not trusting the common sense of the two behind her.

She lifted the latch, opened the door enough for a one eyed view of the hazy blackness outside.

Nobody was there.

She was about to shut the door when she saw what looked like a parcel on the doormat. She turned on the hallway light, opened the door a little wider to cast some light outside and gasped!

On the mat, lay a black cat, unmoving, on its side. A black graduation cap, with a red bow, tied around it, was placed next to the cat...

Grace shut the door, horror engulfed every nerve in her body – this message was directed at her!

Varuna insisted they call the police should an intruder be lurking in the yard.

They sat in numb silence for two hours before a vehicle sped into the driveway.

The voice at the door announced that he was Warrant Officer Venter.

Varuna let him in. They were in a bedraggled, shocked state. He avoided eye contact with them as he muttered, 'ladies, there's no one in the yard. I will remove the dead cat and hope you can get some sleep. Call me if you are in danger.' They stared in disbelief at Warrant Officer Venter, a young man with not an ounce of emotion nor concern.

They locked the door behind him.

That morning the sun struggled to shine a brilliant light.

15

New Beginning

Leaving behind the baggage and pain of the months leading up to their arrival in Australia was necessary to realign their lives for a happy and peaceful future.

The drive to the rural town where Grace was appointed filled them with excitement and an edge of nervousness.

The dark cloud over Grace had lifted.

The wide open spaces, meadows filled with peaceful grazing livestock was the tranquility they needed as two blissful years passed. The townsfolk were cautious at first in their interactions with the newcomers.

Grace won the hearts of her older patients in her compassionate care of their medical needs. She avoided social interactions while Varuna threw herself into community life, becoming a member of the social committee at the local aged-care facility; she baked batches of her favourite scones which she delivered each week for a shared cuppa and wholesome conversation.

Patience set up a youth organisation in the community hall to assist teenagers. Country towns could be a lonely place for youngsters; Patience was welcomed with open arms, she offered homework help, musical and dance evenings, a weekend craft workshop and book club and offered an 'older sister' listening ear to teen angst.

Their departure to Sydney was a difficult one, they promised to visit once a year to check in on the people they had grown to love.

A saddened Varuna said, 'I have made lifelong connections here, and yet my family relationships were fraught with problems. The conundrum of life…'

'Yes, we've been lucky, but one cannot be blinded to Australia's racist past that still impacts on indigenous communities. We faced apartheid, but for a mother to have her children forcibly taken from her, is unforgivably brutal!' Grace looked at life with critical realism.

'Mama Varuna is sad, Grace, let her have her moment,' Patience teased.

Grace began her contract at City Hospital Emergency Department in south-west Sydney with trepidation; she anticipated she would be at the receiving end of a barrage of sexist comments in a metropolitan hospital.

She pondered if her ethnicity too would make her a target for further abuse. Her colleague, an Austrian-born Australian, faced bullying by her male peers, saying it was endemic in medical circles. With maturity on her back, Grace embraced the diverse opportunities available to her in her chosen home country, she stood strong in her capacity to heal the bodies, and minds of her patients.

After a year, Patience needed a place of her own to advance her professional goals. Although this was a painful severing of their living arrangements, Grace and Varuna supported her decision.

City Hospital became Grace's second home until her mother's tragic death.

*   *   *

The receptionist at ER informed her that the patient who had the emergency caesarean; had been discharged. An hour before her shift, she trawled through recent records for the young woman's details. She felt compelled to follow up on this case.

A mobile number and address were located; the possible intrusiveness of calling at this hour, made her second guess going ahead. Hesitation led to countless missed opportunities in her life.

A recorded message greeted her on the other end of the line: *you have reached Virginia Bale, please leave your number and I'll call back soon.*

'Hello Virginia, this is Dr. Sharvin from City Hospital ER calling to check how you are doing and if you are in need of any further medical attention. You may call me at your earliest convenience on 85535533.'

Five minutes later reception rang to inform her Virginia Bale was on the line.

'Thank you so much for ringing Dr. Sharvin, I appreciate it. You were kind and gentle with me the other night.'

'I'm concerned, you had two major stresses that night, do you need additional support.'

'Do you mean like a psychologist?'

'No, not quite, more a friendly social worker to chat to.'

97

'That will be good, I'm staying with my grandmother who doesn't talk much, so it's difficult to share how I feel. I've been sleeping all day and haven't left the house at all.'

'This is a natural reaction to the trauma you experienced. I will get someone to call you to set up a time to meet with you.'

'I'm a bit nervous about new people, is this a person I could trust, do you know them personally? I really don't want to expose myself any more than is necessary for my healing?'

'I would only recommend someone who would work in your interest.'

'Thank you, Dr. Sharvin. Okay, please arrange it. I'm lost and confused right now.'

'A social worker should come over in a day or two. This is my mobile number, should you have any doubts or questions.'

'Thank you.'

Later the next day Grace called Patience to set up a meeting with Virginia.

'There's a possibility, once I confirm with her, that I could see her tomorrow. Don't worry I'll ensure she gets the best attention. *Relax.* Was your evening hectic as usual? Are you smiling more at the young beau in your department?'

'Patience, I am going to pretend I did not hear that, bye.' She hung up on Patience's match-making suggestions and immediately received a text message from her.

Thanks for hanging up on me sis, lighten up, life is short! Chat soon xx

Too much was happening too soon, for her to get tangled in some flighty schoolgirl romance.

Felicity Cassano worked on legal matters pertaining to women of abuse. A lot of her time was devoted to assisting Patience with setting up the *Women in Distress Campaign.* She called Felicity for advice.

Felicity picked up on the third ring.

'Grace, how are you? It has been a while since we last spoke. What's up?'

'Hi Felicity, sorry for falling off the radar, I hope you don't think I only call when I need something, the thing is I need your legal ear on how to proceed with a patient.'

'Shoot, I'm listening.'

She outlined the situation and was happy to note that follow ups and suggestions on the mental and emotional wellbeing of ER patients were within legal expectations.

'I won't mince my words, but are you reaching out to fill your own emotional need or is this a general medical follow up? I suspect it's both.'

Grace drew a deep breath before she responded.

'I'm human, acting in a professional capacity but my conscience has made me reach out more than I would with other patients. She will be receiving support from Patience, and I will slip into the background.'

'I hope so Grace, you must remove yourself, not much is known about the personal situation of this woman. The legal side is not an issue so let's talk later again, once Patience has provided support. On a friendly note, when am I going to see you? You have to get out of hibernation, winter is over!'

'Work has consumed me, but, I have a weekend off at the end of the month, if you're available, it's the Melbourne Cup and it's on a Friday so we could make a long weekend of it. I have more research to conduct before the conference, but a change of scene will be good.' She gabbled on in one breath before Felicity took control of the conversation.

'I hope you don't intend to work then! Let's lock that in, we need a catch up to discuss work *and* our lives. It has been hectic on my end too. I've had quite a few cases, with tensions mounting and our sisters, as always become victims.'

'We need to make an effort to meet more often. Thank you for your advice, I will confirm the flight with Patience.'

'I'm holding you to that promise.'

*　　*　　*

Andrew Lang was in an uncharacteristic sombre mood. He greeted Grace with an air of distant formality. To avoid the awkwardness between them, she retreated to her office to bury herself in a mountain of paperwork. After an hour she walked to his desk.

'Dr. Lang, may I please have the stats on the last patient, the gentleman with the fractures.'

For the first time that evening, Andrew looked at her and responded with a bland, 'he's in recovery now, Dr. Sharvin, I will check in on him again and report back to you.'

Grace felt the chill in his voice, his formality of address suggested he had given up on her, opting for a distant professional, relationship. She had spurned all his advances, she was stoic in avoiding fraternising with the staff she supervised. His cold demeanour bruised her, but she was resolute in maintaining the distance he seemed to want.

An overheard conversation between two nurses in the dispensary explained his mood.

'Poor Andrew, he should not have come in today. He's devastated by the death of his flat mate; it was an awful crash, died instantly, I hear. He is so out of it tonight, Dr. Sharvin should let him go home.'

'Is the ice-maiden aware of his situation? She is too driven by her self-importance to read the signs, even though he's clearly distressed.'

The 'ice-maiden' tag was no surprise to Grace who thought it an unfair, cruel label. How could they judge her this way? She detested gossip, she walked into the dispensing room to let them know she overheard the conversation. Both froze, dumb struck when they saw her, unsure of what she might have heard.

'Good evening Dr. Sharvin.'

'How are you tonight, ladies?'

'We were just talking about the terrible tragedy …'

Grace did not miss the moment to cut in, 'you mean Dr. Lang's flat mate being killed in an accident last night, yes, I heard you as I came in. I will have a word with him, might tell him to go home, that would be the sensible thing to do, right?'

She walked out, leaving them unsure whether she had heard their 'ice-maiden' comment.

Andrew pored over the files on his desk, seeking oblivion and avoiding interactions. He didn't hear Grace walk in.

'May I speak to you for a minute please, Andrew?'

He noticed she dropped the 'Dr.' formality she carried earlier. She half expected one of his usual playful comments, instead, his eyes returned a cold, blank stare.

'Yes sure, what seems to be the matter Dr. Sharvin?'

'I'm sorry about your flat mate's passing, you should go home, you know.'

'How do you know about Fritz's accident? He asked with loaded pain in his defensive, suspicious attitude.

'I overheard nurses in conversation.'

'Hospital grapevine, yes, how I detest it!'

'I recommend you take the night off.'

'Thank you Dr. Sharvin, I need to be at work tonight.'

'How about having dinner with me, during our break then?'

He looked at her with a raised eyebrow, not knowing how to react.

'That's a lovely idea Grace, but aren't you concerned about the hospital grapevine?' He studied her face for a reaction. She smiled, relieved that she was 'Grace' again.

'I'm sure I can support a colleague who has just lost a dear friend, without it being speculated as a sordid activity.'

He managed a smile as he turned on the familiar charm.

'Dr. Sharvin, a brave move indeed, I promise I will not taint your reputation.'

'Thank you, kind sir, I'll see you during dinner. Care to share some of my meal?'

'I won't have much of an appetite, but yes thank you.'

Grace attended to a burn victim as she pondered what Patience would make of this unplanned rendezvous in the hospital dining room.

16

Melbourne Getaway

The early morning flight provided much-needed respite, a change of scene, even if it meant working while she was away was better than being holed-up in her apartment, drowning in work; living on endless cups of coffee and odd cat-naps.

It was a wet weekend in Melbourne, planned outdoor activities were a non-event.

Felicity Cassano and Patience became friends and business associates after meeting at a conference in Sydney ten years ago. They chatted over morning tea, exchanged telephone numbers and struck up a connection in their service to others. They established safe houses in New South Wales, and Melbourne as the *Sisters Helping Sisters Organisation (SHSO)*. Later they set up the *Women in Distress Campaign*. They were in the final stages of having South Australia ready for sisters in distress there. The Western Australia Centre and the safe house were still in the pipeline with the promise of funding from interstate businesses. This would ease up the intensity of their fundraising drives, giving them more time to offer strategic support to women in need.

Felicity was the daughter of migrant parents who came out to Australia from Italy as newly-weds. She was born a year after her parent's arrival in Australia. Her mother died two weeks after she was born – it was a strenuous pregnancy and complicated birth. Her father had a mental breakdown soon after the mother's death leaving her in foster care. Those early challenges shaped the course of her life.

She was a statuesque woman in her mid-fifties with pale, long, golden brown hair that cascaded down her back. Her aquiline nose hinted at a hardness even though her smile was infectious.

She met them at the airport and bundled them off for brunch at *1932 Cafe & Restaurant* on Collins Street, an iconic architectural experience with its 1930 era décor.

Patience could not contain her exuberance as she looked through the menu, squealing with delight that 'Blueberry Vanilla Chia Pudding' was on offer.

Everything was in place for the weekend getaway at a stunning, remote seaside cottage which Felicity rented from a colleague. Grace was not too happy with the intermittent wireless connection, a deliberate choice for more conversations and relaxation.

'We need this seclusion from our hectic schedules, forget about wireless issues, chill and enjoy down time. A catch up on what's going on in our personal worlds is essential. Choose a healthy brekky and you'll feel brand new again.' Felicity did her level best to lift Grace out of her workaholic mindset.

Patience agreed that this was their 'our' time and proposed they spend no more than an hour talking shop.

'Good idea, you are always our common sense. We know how work dominates our conversations. I second that, what about you Grace?'

'Yes, I agree, but I might steal a few hours before you both rise to review my paper.'

'Oh, how are you to relax if you're getting up with the larks?'

Grace ignored the comment not wanting to get her bristles up this early on the trip.

They arrived at the cottage after a long, winding drive along a dirt track. The quaint cottage was surrounded by dense bushland. A swimming pool was not much use to them with the increase in rain that powered down with no end in sight.

'We love cooking together, or if not, sandwiches or a barbecue are just as good.'

'Fifteen minutes to settle and then our 'one hour only' work debrief in the lounge room, girlfriends.'

'You make this sound like a Girls' Scout weekend away Patience!'

'One hour, it shall be, then the fun and games begin. I have everything arranged, I have some Zumba moves up my sleeve to ensure we have the body, mind and spirit experience. Let's hope we can fit in a beach party for three in the rain!' Felicity loved a flexible life, she worked hard and played just as hard.

After unpacking her bag and her laptop, Grace appeared more relaxed after fifteen minutes alone with her thoughts.

*　　*　　*

A platter of an assortment of cold cuts of cured meat, crackers, nuts, and a selection of the finest Australian cheeses with good wine from the Hunter and Barossa valleys set the pace for the afternoon.

Felicity filled them in on the situation at the detention centre.

'The conditions are shocking. Heat and appalling sanitation make it very difficult for our sisters, not that men are any better off. Physical and verbal abuse is escalating, and as you know, psychological issues are on the increase. A lack of adequate ventilation and air cooling systems creates anger, aggression, and illness.'

'Things we take for granted all the time.'

'We are little voices making a few waves for change, but we need more support to extend and grow more safe homes for the sisters.'

'Yeah, the conference brought in some great financial backing from a few businesses. There needs to be ongoing fundraising auctions to sustain the project. Dipping into our private earnings is noble, but cannot go on forever.'

Grace listened in silence before suggesting,

'We need to come up with some ideas on how to enlist support from local doctors. We have many volunteers, from a medical service perspective, but money's needed to keep up with daily expenses.'

'Should we host a dinner-dance as a New Year project? People tend to be generous during that time of year.'

'That might yield generous contributions. We should work on this.'

Patience added, 'it's a great suggestion, but we have to conduct a survey first, to establish how many people will attend as many will be away, on leave and out of the country. What's the situation in your ER centre, Grace?'

'We have a first come quota system for leave requests at this time of year, it's the busiest period for us. I think a Christmas Fund raiser is a marvelous idea.'

Felicity and Patience penned this into their diaries. Their work schedule doubled with that decision, but sisters in difficult situations were their priority.

'Grace, how are things on your front? Will you be able to commit to this project too?'

'Certainly! I would not suggest it if I wasn't going to contribute.'

'The more reliable hands on deck, the more likely we are to succeed in this initiative. I think we should also

consider bringing celebrities on board, sort of something like a celebrity auction. I can look into that.'

'That would yield lots more funds, thanks for the suggestion.' Patience added.

'Glad you support the idea. Now that's settled, let's get personal, so tell me, Grace, how's the handsome male intern, is he still flirting with you?'

Grace shot Patience a look that shouted, *what have you been saying behind my back, sister?'*

'I hope you don't mind, Felicity asked if you were seeing anyone and I told her about Andrew Lang.'

'There's nothing to tell, I'm not 'seeing' him! He's a work colleague.'

'Let's rephrase that, give us all your reasons for spurning the young doctor,' Felicity urged.

'I'm not the only one who's curious, Grace, so spill the beans girlfriend!'

'He is a lovely person deserving a lovely young woman who will enthuse him in his endeavours. I don't have the energy, nor the inclination to start anything with him. How would that look, I'm his supervisor? I will not be reckless and risk losing everything I've worked hard to establish. My reputation means more to me than a one night stand!'

'Yeah, we understand that, but lap up the attention, at least you know you're desirable!' Felicity was impulsive, she had good intentions that often overstepped the mark of friendship. Grace remained calm despite feeling rising irritation.

'I enjoy his company, but will not mislead him by encouraging the friendship.'

'Perhaps you should tell him you want to avoid romantic expectations, then see what he says.' Patience dropped her teasing, taking on a serious, well-intentioned attitude.

'I will think about it. Andrew's in a dark place at the moment with his flat mate's death. We sat together during the dinner break the other night. He was appreciative of the time and attention I gave him.'

'Yeah that's what you should be doing, let people in. It's a way for you to heal from your mother's passing.'

Grace felt a rock was hurled at her with that comment, she paused and summoned her mother's good sense.

'Enough on me now, how about you two? Who are the delights of your lives? I seem to be an open book with you both, so how about you fill me in on *your* secrets.' Grace hated having her life held up for scrutiny; she felt violated, her soul was being revealed without her consent.

*   *   *

The first night was a restless one for Grace. She wafted off into a disturbed sleep. Her body stiffened, then trembled.

Familiar strains of a dreaded lyric grew louder. Rain gushed down… Her hands were drenched and slippery. She struggled to haul her keys out of her handbag. Her remote keypad was sticky in the dampness of a humid night, she fumbled, pushing in the key to unlock the door... the mist descended in its elusive circular dance, surrounding her; the night grew colder. She got in, tossed her bag and umbrella onto the floor on the passenger side; she reached for the towel in the cubbyhole, wiped her face and hands, rubbing her hands together to keep them warm... she turned to place the towel on the passenger seat... she blinked to be sure that she saw a man's face under the hood he wore, peering at her through the window... the person was jimmying the passenger door! She screamed... her voice drowned, fading out...

Grace turned on the bedside lamp and dragged herself to the bathroom. She looked at herself in the mirror, a fear-stricken stranger's face stared back at her. Life was passing by, she was existing rather than participating in life. She stopped her therapy sessions when her mother died, now the cracks were beginning to widen...

17

The Storm

Serene days, close to nature, was the elixir they needed. Relaxed, no ticking clocks, stretched out breakfasts, leisurely bush walks and the promise of a refreshing swim, washed away thoughts of work for Patience and Felicity. Tranquility made Grace vulnerable, her inner voices grew louder. Daylight promised wholesomeness, her nights grew sinister.

Cold, wet nights unnerved her, hindering sleep, making it possible for extended hours of work.. Her disturbed nights remained undisclosed, she avoided upsetting Felicity's mood and plans. Stealing away for an hour each day under the pretext of working, helped her get a quick shut-eye to sustain her energy.

Night storms lashed across the state, making her restless and melancholic. Her mounting fears and dreams forced her to acknowledge she needed professional help.

At midnight while Felicity and Patience slept, she slipped

out into the storm. Dressed in a pair of black pants and a white t-shirt, she held her face up to the lashing wind and rain. She yelled with as much force as she could muster, 'out, out you blasted demons! I want to feel whole again!'

Within seconds she was drenched to the skin, a bedraggled, pitiful mess… Her water-saturated hair, dripped down her face, blurring her vision. She had been silent for too long, the surging voices within cried out for release.

'Cleanse me! Cleanse this sullied, tainted body!'

She walked around in a zombie-trance, digging her feet into the soft, mushy ground, releasing all she kept bottled up. She sobbed like a child lost in the wilderness of a night storm.

Patience awoke to the crashing sound of thunder and flashing lightning. She strolled to the kitchen for a glass of water. Another blinding flash of lightning lit up the front yard, she saw Grace huddled on the ground. She woke Felicity up to gather blankets and towels, she had to bring her sister out of the storm.

A gentle, steady hand, on her shoulder, made her tremble… Patience stood beside her, face contorted with fear and tears. She sat on the ground with Grace, cradling her head in her lap with the maternal affection of their mothers.

Felicity stayed indoors, watching from the kitchen window, waiting for the calming of this cathartic moment. Grace was a desolate figure, hanging onto Patience as she guided her back to the cottage. Felicity rummaged through the laundry cupboard and found a large heater. They sat around the heater, sipping tea in silence.

Grace sat staring without blinking, her mind blank, frozen in the moment.

Unable to bear the stillness any longer, Felicity said, 'what possessed you to go walking out in the storm tonight?'

Patience pressed Grace's hand, in a very soft voice she said, 'later Felicity, later, Grace needs to rest and keep warm. We can sit here together for now.'

Nature heightened and unleashed her trapped storm, leaving her hapless, as the people closest to her, watched on, concerned and afraid.

*   *   *

Grace prepared herself for Felicity's questions and assumptions on the state of her mental health. A new wave of tension gripped her, she was not ready to bare her soul. Patience was sensible in not asking probing questions.

Felicity, the self-appointed meals 'advocate' for the weekend, enjoyed watching others savour her meals. She reluctantly promised herself, she would not push to know why Grace acted out of character last night.

'Grace, I hope you're up to cooking your delicious chicken curry tonight. I brought some flat-bread and pickles along so let me know how I can help.'

Grace struggled to summon an excited voice.

'I'd love to prepare dinner tonight, I find cooking therapeutic. Shall we make it a team effort? You've been asking me, for many years, to demonstrate making a curry, so let's do that together.'

'Wonderful, I need to sharpen and vary my cooking skills, a joint venture it shall be! I brought spices along, cumin, cardamom, chilli powder and ground ginger and garlic. I know the bare essentials of a South African curry but need to master the fine art. So what am I missing?'

'Coriander, curry leaves and a pinch of garam masala add to the flavour, but a spicy curry with what you have is possible.'

'What is 'garam masala? Can I buy it at the Indian store in Melbourne?'

'You can, but mum, god bless her, taught me to grind my own. I will send you some when I get back home. Its fresher and aromatic with greater Ayurvedic benefit.'

Patience listened, gauging that Grace was in a better frame of mind which allowed her to tease her sister again.

'Hey doc, Ayurvedic healing? No pharmaceutical drugs today?' She laughed her infectious laugh that brought the house down. She knew Grace attached great value to natural healing and only prescribed drugs in dire circumstances.

'In nature, it has to be 'nature's way," Grace added, letting them know they did not have to tip-toe around her.

*   *   *

Around midnight, after a hearty combination of chicken curry, bread, and pickles, it was time for soulful conversation. The gods smiled down on them that night — no storm, just a windy night which sent the wind chimes on the veranda into a spiral gyration. The melodic tinny and glassy sounds soothed their frayed nerves.

Grace cleared her throat in nervous anticipation of the response she would receive from what she was about to say.

'I cannot thank you both enough for helping me through last night. I'm experiencing burn-out, I've been working with not much time off since mum's passing. Am I coping? No, but I'm happiest when I'm helping others. The decision I've come to after some soul searching, is that I need professional help, I will see Dr. Deakin again — the baggage is weighing me down...' She said this in one breath, looking out the window as she spoke, ashamed that *dependable, hardworking Grace* was a failure. Her legs twitched as she took a deep breath and continued, 'you both have been wonderful, it's time I worked on myself with the help of an objective professional.'

'It will make a world of difference! You won't know your-self.' Patience's exuberant acknowledgment looked beyond what Grace considered her failing, all she wanted was her sister to be whole and happy again.

Felicity nodded in agreement with a troubled, analytical gaze at Grace.

'You must not block anything that has disturbed you over the years, you must take Dr. Deakin into your complete trust. We both want you to feel joyful again. Take leave from work to get your life in order.'

Grace appreciated Felicity's thoughtfulness but resented her dictating tone and suggestion that she should take leave from work to 'get her life in order.'

'I'll begin the sessions with Dr. Deakin and see how I go, it's a busy time at my work.'

Felicity could be pushy, sometimes unable to pick up the cues of resistance to her suggestions.

'You need to look after **YOU**, Grace. I can't spell it out any more.'

Patience jumped in, 'she is doing that Felicity by starting with seeing Dr. Deakin. I'm sure Grace will know at some point if leave is necessary for her wellbeing.'

Felicity's hard life had given her a thick skin. Her tenacious-ness in coping with life's challenges made her insensitive to Grace's problems. She thrived on helping others, had influence in getting Patience on the road with her campaign for the safe-houses yet she always expected more from Grace.

Patience understood the challenges Grace went through in their years in South Africa, there was a part that Grace guarded, not letting anyone in, not even her mother.

The drive back to Melbourne was a slow, relaxed drive. They had an early morning flight back to Sydney. Felicity turned on the car radio, she enjoyed belting out songs, on road trips. She flicked through radio stations settling on *smoothfm 91.5*

Grace stiffened, the song playing, was familiar; it was the song in her dream. She leaned forward, almost diving over Felicity, in her scramble to turn off the radio.

'What on earth are you doing, Grace?' Felicity yelled, 'I almost lost control of the wheel with your sudden lunge. You could have asked me to turn it off if the music was not to your taste.'

Patience touched Felicity on the shoulder to stop her rant.

Grace sat rigid, transfixed, eyes, wide and staring, not hearing a word Felicity was saying.

'Felicity, we need to stop when its safe, I need to get Grace out the car for a while, please stop at a safe clearing or at one of the roadside filling stations.'

Felicity still shocked by what had just happened, agreed to stop. The freeway was busy with people rushing home after a long weekend. It dawned on her that the song had triggered a painful memory for Grace. She knew South Africa was a violent country and yearned to understand what had rattled Grace.

She pulled up at a clearing off the road. A table and bench were nestled among trees. Patience guided Grace to the seat. She was withdrawn, silent and tired.

They spoke in lowered tones, until Grace's equilibrium returned.

Felicity's agitation and concern pushed her into doing the unthinkable. She made a call while watching Grace and Patience in earnest conversation.

'Dr. Deakin, its Felicity Cassano. Not sure if you remember me. I'm an acquaintance of Dr. Grace Sharvin. I'm concerned about Grace. It appears she is having a breakdown. You should call her when she gets back home, I fear something awful might happen to her.'

'Thank you Ms. Cassano, I appreciate your concern. Grace or her next of kin will have to contact me, I cannot call her and explain I am acting on your referral. I hope you understand what I'm saying. We cannot let our emotions get the better of us. I know you are acting out of concern but suggest you leave it up to Dr. Sharvin.'

Felicity watched them return to the car. She had to keep silent about her call to Dr. Deakin.

Grace apologised for delaying the trip home. Not another word was uttered for the rest of the drive to Melbourne.

They booked at a hotel, close to the airport to avoid dense morning traffic from Felicity's St Kilda apartment.

Felicity was irritable and edgy that she was not privy to what had troubled Grace. Curiosity pushed her to probe further, 'when are you going to explain what happened in the car?'

'This is not the right time to expect an explanation, Felicity, can we leave it there for now?' Patience felt compelled to assume guardianship over her sister once again to protect her pride and dignity.

They exchanged a cool goodbye. Patience dreaded the badgering she would get from Felicity for a detailed recount of their conversation on the bench, in the middle of nowhere.

18

Façade

Grace welcomed a busy night in ER to get her back into the swing of life in an environment she had greater control over — the hospital was her safe haven.

Andrew Lang approached her with his customary, fetching smile.

'How was your weekend in Melbourne Dr. Sharvin? You are glowing!'

'Hello Andrew, please drop the formality. Nowhere near glowing, I assure you! Too many hours away and I'm paying with a backlog of catch-up work I have to do.'

'A break helps to sharpen perspective, Grace. You work way too hard.'

'You sound like the voices I heard this weekend!' She smiled not wanting Andrew to see how stressed she really was.

'How are you? Any news on Fritz's funeral yet?'

'Thank you for asking. His sister has come forward to assist me with the funeral arrangements. He was estranged from his family but kept in touch with his sister.'

'You have a lot on your shoulders. Are you coping with all that's been thrust upon you?'

'I am coping well now thanks, after the initial shock. Work helps me forget. Fritz was more than a flat mate, he was like an older brother. We spent lots of evenings chatting about life, our hopes and dreams, I feel the void. I'm not ready to find another boarder and have considered not having one at all.'

'Yeah, I know that feeling, I felt it after my mum passed on. You need to mourn in private — losing friends or family, is the hardest pain to bear, it runs deep to the core of your being. Let me know if there's anything I can help you with.'

'You've got a lot happening now, thank you, your listening ear is all I need.'

'Let's hope we don't have too many casualties tonight.'

'It does seem to have quietened down after last weekend.'

They spent an hour going through, updating and following up on their patients.

Grace received a paramedic message that staff from a city restaurant, involved in an explosion in the kitchen, were being brought in.

Grace was back in the saddle, she picked up the microphone and announced:

'All hands on deck, kitted please, gas explosion victims arriving in three minutes!'

Wheelchairs, wheelie beds, masks, gloves, and over-shoes were gathered with speed. Staff knew Grace was a medical Nazi about keeping their unit sterile. Everybody stood to attention when Grace made an announcement.

Six patients were attended to, with Grace in the front line, cleaning, bandaging, calming and soothing. She worked side-by-side with her staff. Her work ethic and personal motto were to work with speed and efficiency to ease the pain of others. This brought negative criticism from some of her colleagues who perceived her to be a micro-manager. Six months ago she addressed this with them when she was challenged by a group of young interns.

Human life meant 'all hands on deck' to save lives. She made it very clear that micro-management perceptions had no place in the saving of lives and healing in her ER facility. She knew her forthright manner was not well received, she had to be true to her life mission. One casualty had burns to seventy percent of her body. Grace moved her to intensive care for specialised treatment. Her impaired breathing suggested there might be lung damage.

That night, Andrew Lang proved he was reliable and dedicated to saving lives. The thing that annoyed Grace the most was when staff spoke to patients with a cold business tone and attitude. She worked hard to change the values and mindset in her team, but every now and then a new intern came in as an upstart. Her strength was her marriage to her profession, anyone who dared mistreat a patient had her wrath to deal with.

Grace was an indomitable force on her work front – her private world churned, going undetected by most, concealed in her artful, composed façade.

*   *   *

Dr. Deakin fitted Grace in at noon the next day. She was sleep-deprived, restless and fearful that her privacy was about to be invaded.

Dr. Deakin, a slender, short woman, was in her late forties. Her mane of shoulder-length, straight, dark-brown hair and penetrating green eyes unnerved Grace, each time she saw her.

She knew she had to come to terms with her demons by not holding back on vital information. The last few visits before Varuna passed away, was to help her cope with burn-out. She was hell-bent on protecting her dignity. Revealing her fears, exposing her weakness and failures added to her anxiety.

'Hello Grace, good to see you again.' She appreciated the warm, maternal tone, pride gripped her sensibilities once again, reconstructing her protective wall.

'Good day Dr. Deakin,' was her formal, impenetrable response, 'thank you for seeing me at short notice.'

'Did you have a busy night?'

'Not really, other weeks have been crazy.'

'Did you have a relaxing time away?'

Grace paused, confused that Dr. Deakin knew about her weekend in Melbourne.

'How did you know I was away?'

'I thought you mentioned it when you called.' Dr. Deakin slipped up with revealing information about her that she did not share.

'No, I don't recall doing so.'

Dr. Deakin was awkward, knowing she should not unsettle Grace into clamming up and leaving.

She handed Grace a questionnaire on her physical and emotional understanding of herself. She studied her face noting she looked drained and much thinner than she recalled.

'I see the dreams are back, tell me; when did they start?'

'I'm not too sure, to be honest. Night storms seem to intensify them. My mother's car accident was on a stormy day.'

'What's your workload like?'

'Busy with preparation on a paper for an international conference, so that encroaches on my sleep time too.'

'I suspect you are working on this during the day, working the night shift at ER and working on your days off too.'

'Pretty much. I think not having my mother around to attend to some of my needs has taken its toll. I should not be saying that at forty-five, I suppose.' She rolled her eyes in shame as she articulated how dependent she was on her mother.

'With your treacherous schedule, you need a little help on the home front, I daresay. Any love interest these days? ' Dr. Deakin was careful in slipping this in before Grace closed off from further probing questions. Of all her cases, Grace was the most difficult. Her personal and professional barricade inhibited exposure of vital information Dr. Deakin required.

She chose her words with care, not wanting to seem anxious that she had not found love yet, 'not a love interest but a young intern is trying to gain my attention which I won't succumb to, he's too young and I'm his supervisor.'

'Age is of no consequence these days, but I understand your reservation on professional grounds. It won't hurt to strike up a friendship at least.'

'We have when his roommate died in a motorcycle accident. I suppose it made us kindred spirits.'

Dr. Deakin proceeded with considered care in bringing down the wall that trapped Grace from love and joy.

'That's good, you've connected with him. How are things with your staff these days, are they cooperative?'

'Yes, the new staff seem a dedicated bunch, no complaints there.'

Grace's brief responses meant a new line of questioning was necessary to keep her talking.

'Any particularly interesting cases come up recently?' Dr. Deakin kept this first session work-related, to make Grace comfortable enough, to let down her inhibitions on private matters.

'There was a young woman who was assaulted by her partner, she ended up losing her unborn baby. My sister has taken on the case to assist her with care and finances if she needs it.'

'It's a great service to women who go unnoticed in these circumstances. You are working in the face of human struggles which adds more pressure to your already heavy load.'

'It's good for me too, to get my sister involved. I will follow through with whatever else I can. Felicity Cassano, my sister's legal assistant is preparing for the interstate placement of women, although she is busy with the detention centre issues at the moment.' Dr. Deakin made note of Grace's open willingness to speak about what Patience was working on.

'You are all doing great work, I hope the government sits up and acknowledges the contributions migrants make to this country rather than suggest that migrants are a problem.' They laughed. Dr. Deakin cranked up the level of questioning when Grace began to relax.

'We spoke of hypnosis the last time I saw you. How do you feel about taking that step?'

'A little anxious, but not closed off to the idea. Can we continue with our conversations and decide on that later?'

'No rush at all, only when you're comfortable and ready to do so Grace.'

'Thank you for your understanding.'

'Once we are able to deduce what's locked in your emotional psyche, you will find restful sleep, I'm sure of that. Do you need any sleeping pills? Well, Dr. Sharvin, I should not be asking a medical doctor who is an advocate for natural medicine such a question!' Dr. Deakin remembered their earlier conversations on Grace's reservation on allopathic treatment. This loosened the conversation between client and therapist.

'We shall get to the bottom of this, to restore your peace. It might be a slow process.'

'That will be a dream come true, that's not intended to provide comic relief, it's been too long, I'm exhausted. Whatever it takes, please release me from his prison.'

'Are you able to keep an active journal of all the nights you've felt disturbed? Write down any memory that surfaces. This way we might get a speedier result for you.'

'Yes, shifting my thinking away from my research during those troubled times will be a better option for me.'

'I believe my receptionist informed you that I've booked you at eleven o' clock for the next six Saturday mornings. I hope that suits your calendar.'

'That seems perfect, I leave for Amsterdam in two and a half months, thanks once again.'

Grace stepped out onto the street, Dr. Deakin's office was on the quieter side of town, a few people walked about, and some nodded a greeting to passers-by, creating a friendly air of acknowledgment, unlike the bustling upper north end. Her phone rang somewhere in the crevices of her large handbag.

'Hey Grace, its Felicity, how's things? Did you have a better night? I called Patience when I couldn't reach you at home. She said you were out. Is everything okay? Not like you, to be out and about after your night shift.'

She wished she had not picked up the call. Felicity meant well, her manner was meddlesome. She struggled to be polite.

'Everything is just perfect, I had a few errands to run, as you do. I can't talk, I'm on the way to the car, chat some other time soon.' Grace cut her off to avoid aggravating, prying questions.

An eerie chill surrounded her on her walk through the carpark. The parking lot was empty, it was two o' clock in the afternoon, the sun loomed overhead... she gasped as she reached for the door, a terrified cat scuttled out from under her car.

All five senses were on edge, her neck was stiff, and her back ached.

19

Privacy

Grace was a restless beast contemplating how she would approach Patience with the violation of her privacy. A telephone chat was easier than a face-to-face confrontation.

'I'm so glad to catch you.'

'Hi, you okay? How was your shift?'

'Yeah, not too busy, for some reason we seem to have more burn victims these days, minor cases and some needing high care.'

'Which only you can administer with such dedication Gracie!'

'Letting you know, in confidence, I took the leap and went to see Dr. Deakin today.'

'I'm happy to hear that, how are you feeling after seeing her?'

'It's early days yet, I have to consider whether I will continue with regular sessions, but something she said is bothering me, I want to clear this up with you.'

Patience listened a little shocked at Grace's sudden change in tone.

'What's this about?'

'I won't beat around the bush — it was rather strange that Dr. Deakin asked me about my weekend trip, yet I did not mention it when I called her to set up a meeting.'

'I hope you don't think I said anything. I have not seen nor heard from Dr. Deakin since Mama Varuna passed away, I last saw her when she attended the funeral service.'

'Phew! That's a relief, I knew you would not call her, but needed that confirmation. Do you know whether Felicity called her while we were in Melbourne?'

'Apart from her saying you ought to go back to your therapist, she has said nothing else to me. I could ask her Grace.'

'No that won't be necessary, it was her. Dr. Deakin was quick to say I mentioned the weekend which I didn't. I figured she was covering up something or protecting the source. At least she's human, but it has made me wary about trusting her.'

'Felicity can be impulsive when she thinks she is acting in someone's best interest. I'm sorry this has happened.'

'You're not to blame. I understand, but this is a breach of our friendship if she does this without asking first. God knows what else she's said.'

'To put your mind at ease you should question Dr. Deakin on the matter. She is a respected professional and would not deliberately sabotage a client's confidentiality.'

'I agree. Sorry to unburden on you, I do it all the time, but I will ask her in an appropriate moment.'

'I'm glad you're considering doing so. Do you want to hear what happened to me?'

'Is it something Felicity has done?'

'No, no, I had a nasty incident this morning, or rather, an

unnerving incident, a call from an estranged husband of a woman placed in the safe house here. He demanded knowing where she was, called me an unmentionable, interfering individual and proceeded to tell me that's why I don't have a man in my life. He must be watching me or gathering information on me. I brushed it aside as an irate partner who cannot deal with his wife's absence, at least she's out of harm's way.'

'You should alert the police. There are so many crazies out there. Please be careful.'

'I'll come over on Thursday, after work, we can prepare dinner together. Will it be disruptive to your research?'

'Not at all, it's encouragement for me to get more done, before then, to free me for the evening. Cooking dinner with you is not something I'm going to pass up!'

It was the first time she saw Grace's fears manifest on the night of the raging storm. She knew her sister was an introvert who felt aggrieved when people pried into her life. Her mother explained many times that Felicity was not to blame for being impulsive, she lived most of her growing up, shunted from one foster home to another.

Grace accepted that absence of strong familial bonds could have contributed to Felicity's urgency to rectify every troubled situation she came across.

She knew she could never speak about her inner challenges to Felicity who sat in judgement of her, expecting more at every turn by questioning her faults.

*   *   *

Grace heard the crashing sound of glass from the apartment above her. Mrs. Beresford, her upstairs neighbour, was in Canada or was she back, Grace wondered? She had lost track of when she was due back in Sydney. The sensible thing to do was to go upstairs to check on her. As she was about to set out of her apartment, the telephone rang, a wheezy Mrs. Beresford was on the line.

'Hello Grace, I'm back, got in this morning, you must have been asleep or out, I rang your doorbell to let you know I was back. I knew you would be worried if you heard lots of movement from up here…' She broke off, coughed and continued without a pause for Grace to get a word in.

'How are you doing? Didn't get yourself married while I was away now, did you?'

Grace laughed, 'Mrs. Beresford, lovely to know you're home, I was about to come up to check on the noise and to see if you were indeed back. No, foot-loose and fancy free as ever!'

'Glad to hear it, my dear. You sound very cheery so you must be well.'

'I am, thank you. Patience is coming over for dinner tonight, would you like to join us? Its curry night but I could grill salmon and roast veggies for you.'

'I am quite exhausted but have no food in the house until I shop tomorrow morning. Dinner with you will be splendid. I eat curries, you know, as long as it's not too pungent. Don't worry about grilling salmon for me.' She coughed again.

'I'll send Patience to bring you down to dinner when she arrives.'

'That's lovely of you, my dear, give me a tinkle five minutes before she comes up, please.'

'Will do. See you soon. Good to know you're upstairs again. I won't be so lonely now.' Her warm voice and caring nature reminded Mrs. Beresford of her mother. Honouring Varuna, made Grace happy, she assumed the baton of a caring neighbour, something that would have made her mother proud.

Patience arrived at six o' clock with lamb, chicken, and fish.

'That's too much Patience,' Grace complained, knowing that Patience needed to curb her generosity.

'I'm in the mood for a curry feast! They won't take long to cook. Chicken, lamb and fish curry on a weekday night! How exciting! If I have a blood transfusion, your hospital will have to add curry powder to the tubes, to get me on my feet again.' Patience laughed at her own musings, spreading her happy spirit. Her carefree nature was enviable.

Soft jazz piano strains played in the background as they sipped on a cold glass of pinot noir.

'Oh no, I forgot, Mrs. Beresford is joining us for dinner, will you bring her down please Patience?'

'The old biddy is home then? Have you seen her?'

'Not yet, she called to say she's here, very considerate of her. Now that the curries and steamed rice are ready, you should get her. I have to let her know you're coming up.'

Grilled salmon as a back-up dish, was her considerate gesture if the curries were unpalatable for her neighbour. She spruced up the dining table and poured a glass of wine for their visitor.

Mrs. Beresford embraced Grace in a loving bear hug.

'Oh, you are more like your mum now. Darling, caring Varuna. I miss her.'

'We all do, Mrs. Beresford, but we are delighted to have you break bread with us tonight. A glass of white with your salmon should relax you, after your flight back.'

'Thank you, my dear. Soothing music too, just what I need.'

She devoured the curried fish saying it was as flavoursome as the dish she ate many years ago when she visited Goa with her late husband.

'You have your mother's touch there, with the delicate spicing, what a scrumptious meal. Thank you for inviting me over.'

Over a fruit salad and ice-cream dessert, Mrs. Beresford rattled on about her children and how grown-up her grandchildren were. She said Canada was still a beautiful country and just as multi-cultural as Australia. Both Grace and Patience listened with enthusiasm and asked her a million questions.

They were tidying up the kitchen when they heard slow, heavy breathing.

Mrs. Beresford was sitting in the lounge chair, her head was lowered and her chin rested on her chest. Her soft, satisfied snore, accompanied by a few content purring sounds indicated she was in a deep sleep.

'Well, I suppose we're all going to be that way, someday. Mama Varuna was something else though, she was so alert and hip and happening. We should strive to be the same at her age. Her cheerful disposition must never be forgotten.'

'Absolutely, she was a live-wire, I miss her so much.'

Grace lifted Mrs Beresford's legs to a comfortable position on the couch, she placed a cushion behind her head and draped a soft cashmere blanket over her.

'I won't disturb her, she can stay over. The wine sent her nodding off, poor thing, she said she was exhausted.'

'Yeah, it's best not to disturb her. Following in Mama's footsteps will add to our good karma.'

'Well, are we doing it because we care or because we want to reap the cosmic benefits of being kind? That is the question, sister dear!'

'Come on, you know what I mean.'

They both did some serious maturing in the last year.

Grace considered, then hesitated giving Patience an inkling on the reason for her breakdown in Melbourne; she decided, it would have to wait until another day. Patience accepted the offer to stay over that night, she outlined how she planned to assist Virginia in reclaiming her life.

'To quote Virginia, you are a 'silent, caring angel'.'

'I felt her pain, I've never experienced this with other patients. I never veer from professionalism, but Virginia tugged at my heart strings, she's so young to have gone through so much.'

'You are a doctor with a big, caring heart and there's nothing wrong with that, a dose of kindness saves many lives.'

'On that note, did you report the threatening call you received, to the police?'

'I did, please promise, you won't worry about this now. I will be fine.'

Grace's anxiety was spiralling out of control, she struggled to conceal it.

There were hidden chambers within her, in desperate need of light.

20

Looking for Answers

Ahopeful, sunburst sky, unanswered questions and awk-ward acknowledgement of what peeved her, governed Grace's thoughts on her way to her second appointment with Dr. Deakin.

'Good morning Grace, what a lovely day it is. I wish I could get outdoors for a walk later today.'

'It certainly is a glorious day, bright and beautiful. You should take some time to get out if you can.'

'How are you feeling after the last session?'

'Better, I think.' If there was one thing Grace abhorred, it was a dalliance, she got right to it, hoping she would not be perceived as attacking her therapist.

'There is something I want to get off my chest.'

'What is it Grace?' Dr. Deakin raised a concerned eyebrow and lowered her head in her usual pensive manner. She knew

Grace bottled up her thoughts and feelings. It was rare that she would volunteer what troubled her.

'Did Felicity Cassano call you during the weekend we were away, that is the Melbourne Cup long weekend?'

'I must admit she did, in asking me to see you. She is a concerned friend but I set her straight by telling her it was against my professional ethics to act on her assumptions without consulting you.'

'I see, has she called you again?'

'No, I won't be entertaining her calls, it will be counterproductive to what I wish to achieve with you. She caught me off guard with her call. I don't remember meeting her, she seems to know me.'

'I needed to clear this, it troubled me as I knew I did not tell you I was away. My poor sister faced an interrogation on this. Your response is what I needed to hear. Perhaps it's just me, but, I can't function if I feel my trust has been violated.'

'Certainly, I could not agree more, a relationship with a therapist is based on trust. I hope you understand, its better you found out this way, rather than me putting a wedge between you two. I'm in the business of mending relationships too!' Dr. Deakin's explanation attempted to soften the situation, her last comment did not go down too well with Grace, leaving her pondering how on earth it was possible to compromise truth, to save relationships.

'Thank you, I do, I have no intention of letting this ruin the friendship with Felicity. It would have spared me the doubt of my sister's involvement, had I known this from the outset.' Grace's intensity and final acceptance of the situation signalled her expectations on privacy and truthfulness.

'Now that we've cleared that, let's start over with no misunderstandings.'

'Thank you.'

'If you're ready, let's begin. Have you had more of those recurring dreams?'

'No, I haven't. It could be because I had Patience stay over the other night and we had a dinner guest; my mind was preoccupied with external stimuli, I suppose.'

'Your self-reflection is amazing. Let's talk about the person in your dream. I will commence with my questions now.' Her warm, gentle voice soothed Grace, washing away her irritation, like a warm caramel latte.

'Take a deep breath and relax. Think of it as recalling a distant memory.'

'I feel the figure is a male person in his twenties, the gait and stature suggest that he is.'

'Was he in any way familiar?'

Grace paused, fixing her eyes on a painting of huge grey waves crashing against craggy black rocks on the wall in front of her, before responding. She delved within, prodding her memory for answers. Shaking her head, exasperated, she said, 'I can't be sure, I can't quite see the face because of the hood. The music was familiar, not so much the words... the music was familiar.'

'Let's focus on the music. Was it fast or slow?'

'It was slow... I think it was a romantic song.'

'Where might you have heard it before?'

Grace shut her eyes, squeezing them together into a fine-lined map of wrinkles, 'I feel I heard it played before at some gathering. 'It's so foggy. I can almost feel it's there but not quite, does that make sense?'

'As a fellow professional, I can tell you this, fear caused by trauma can often block memory in a subconscious way. It's our coping mechanism. Take note when these dreams occur, I would think they surface when you are stressed or exposed to stimuli that connect with your dream. I have a few memory exercises for you to conduct at home, but first, I need you to tell me a little more about the song? Was it a contemporary song, one that is popular?'

'No it was older, from another era, I think. Perhaps my parents played it, I'm not sure...'

'The exercises will involve listening to some music to nudge your memory into recalling the details of the night in question. Have you been listening to any particular type of music in recent weeks?'

'No, not anything specific for any length of time, apart from the smooth jazz grooves that Patience played when we had dinner together on Thursday. I don't listen to music when I'm alone at home, I need to hear the sounds that come from outside my apartment. Things are not safe anymore, one has to be alert to danger.'

Dr. Deakin made copious notes on Grace's escalated anxiety and her unwarranted concerns for her safety. Grace had slipped beyond work burnout, she was rapidly descending into a dark mental space. She advised her to listen to music from a playlist she selected, before going to bed and to record any emotional triggers that arose.

Grace accepted this would stretch her already overcrowded 'to do list,' but it was time to exorcise her demons.

*   *   *

The sight of Mrs. Beresford being wheeled into an ambulance greeted Grace on her return from therapy. She approached the paramedic to allow her to ride with her to the hospital.

'Oh Grace, thank god, you're here. I got out the shower and slipped on the rug, I don't know why this happened, the searing pain on my left side makes me feel faint. Grace spoke to the paramedic explaining that Mrs. Beresford might need a little morphine to ease her pain.

'We have no medical history on the patient, do you know her well?'

'Just as my upstairs neighbour, I have no specific personal medical history.'

Grace settled Mrs. Beresford at the hospital and promised to look in on her. She would have to solicit assistance from Patience in offering a level of care and support as the only way to juggle all she had on her plate.

'Hi Patience, Mrs. B had a fall this morning, both her hips are fractured. I need help with hospital visits until we can figure out what care she would need.'

'I could help on some days, what about contacting her children in Canada?'

'Thanks, Patience. I have no contact details for her children, I'll get it off her tomorrow.'

'I'll pop in to see her in a few hours and get those details, we have to let them know as soon as possible. Perhaps one of her children could come out to be with her.'

'We can try, in all the time we've been living in the apartment, they've never visited her. She goes out every couple of years to see her grandchildren.'

'I'll send you a message later, get some sleep now, before your shift tonight.'

'Hope to, chat later.'

*　　*　　*

A warm bath with a splash of the sweet, spicy aroma of Frankincense, alleviated the stressful beginning of the day. She thought of Mrs. Beresford and hoped she was not in too much pain.

After a warm cup of almond, honeyed milk, she drew the heavy curtains across her bedroom window and balcony sliding door, blocking out a cerulean skyline.

The song she selected from the playlist was familiar, she hummed along. Her eyelids drooped, letting in slivers of light into her artificial night, drowning her waking senses.

She was a voyeur of her own dream, one that had haunted her for almost two decades. It was back with a vengeance, hunting her down, breaking her, forcing her to submit to remembrance.

The figure continued the frenzied tug at the car door, she froze, her mind paralysed, she stared at the hooded figure outlined in the mist and rain. Her voice crippled with fear. The clanging sound of metal, grinding and scratching deafened her. She reached for her handbag to retrieve her mobile phone.

The bag was open, the contents had fallen out onto the floor of the car.

It was pitch black – she dared not make a run for it.

The song played on, in its slow, seductive, rhythmic croon, her heart hammered, her pulse a crescendo in her ears… the door opened… he looked at her with a maddening inferno in his eyes.

The song continued its torment. She slumped onto the steering wheel, the hooter blared an endless cry into the emptiness of the night…

Grace woke up with a bolt when her alarm went off at five o' clock. She lay in bed for another half hour, uneasy about facing the night. Her shift was a daunting thought — taking a sick day off crossed her mind, she squashed the idea and prepared a hurried cup of *Rooibos* tea and a toasted cheese sandwich.

The memory of her dream surfaced when she got into the

car, dread coursed through her body. The face of the hooded figure was hard to ignore. She sat in the car, looked at the passenger window and closed her eyes, willing herself to remember more. Soon there was a tapping, on the driver side window. She let out a blood curdling scream — the shocked building janitor stood horrified at the window, asking her what had happened and if he could help her. Grace was too embarrassed to say anything, she raised her hand in a thank you gesture, started the car and drove off. The janitor watched her leave, shaking his head in disbelief.

She arrived earlier than expected at the hospital and voice recorded what she remembered from her dream.

Her mother's soothing, humming words returned from her early childhood, the words she awoke to, in tears, after a terrifying dream.

You are not alone, I'm with you as you sleep. Look at the bright moon smiling down at you; the stars twinkle to let you know they are watching over you, you are not alone. Sleep child... sleep.

21

Good Neighbour

The evening air was dank, beads of perspiration formed on Grace's chin and brow. The heat had a strange influence on people — ER was always overcrowded on a hot night. People seemed more accident prone or aggressive towards each other on balmy nights. Add substance abuse and the stats multiplied. She pondered why people gravitated towards inhumanity when a little self-control and kindness saved untold atrocities.

Andrew waved a greeting across the hallway when he saw her enter. She waved back in regal gesture.

Blue floors, pale grey walls, florescent lighting and white coats washed away her troubles. This was her safe space where external thoughts had no place.

Half an hour after her arrival, Andrew walked over to her room with a cup of coffee.

'How are you tonight Grace, you seem preoccupied, every-thing okay?'

'Hi Andrew, thanks for noticing, just a lot on my mind.'

'Anything I can help you with?'

'Not really, but thanks anyway. My upstairs neighbour, an elderly woman, had a fall today and I've spent part of my day admitting her to the local private hospital. What an amazing facility. I'm glad she's getting good care, she has no family here in Sydney.'

'Is it your presumption that patients only get good care in private hospitals? I am inclined to disagree, if this is what you're suggesting, you do one heck of a job, in your medical and per-sonal care of patients who arrive broken and leave grateful.'

'You are way too kind, I wish that was a hundred percent true, some don't make it out of here... but, some things are beyond human control. We may be blessed with a human touch, the most important part of our jobs, but we are understaffed and ill-equipped. Have you seen the new stock of arm slings that came in? Well, let me tell you, they are stiff as sandpaper and the clasp is a clunky metal hoop. Its capable of causing skin abrasions and will not offer much relief from pain, and that's one example of the inferior products we receive.'

'Yeah I know we are lacking in that area, it's about cutting costs to the disadvantage of some hospitals.

Location, location, some are more inferior to others. All the lobbying we've done to improve this seems to go unheard. Your good heart does not go unnoticed, though.'

'Enough with the flattery, thank you for the coffee. You better get back to your work or soon prying eyes will lead to wayward thoughts and wagging tongues... who knows what or why people surmise about things they do not understand.' Grace stopped herself from saying anything that might give

Andrew ideas about getting too close to her. She studied his face and saw an earnest, handsome, dedicated doctor. He never let on whether he was in a relationship or out of one.

'Yes, I should, the last thing I want is to create a problem with gossip around what is not happening. Hospital grapevines can be lethal.' He looked at her with a magnetic intensity, sending a shiver down her spine.

'To think we are in the business of saving lives and yet our words are knives that bruise and destroy.' Grace was inclined to become philosophical when situations made her irate.

'Wow, that's poetic Grace!'

He smiled his mesmerising smile and sauntered out.

She watched him walk away, restless, pondering on the cruelty of fate, in placing before her, an almost perfect man who had to remain untouchable. Exhaustion left her light-headed, she trawled through her emails. One caught her attention – it was from Virginia Bale, the young woman who lost her baby, requesting to meet her for coffee. She had to think about how to respond, and decided to leave it to after her shift.

An array of cuts, burns, swollen, punched-up faces, broken teeth, stab wounds and a gunshot victim entered that night. A fight had broken out after a football match, an argument over which team was more skilled. The gunshot victim was semi-conscious. Fifteen minutes in, she heard Andrew call out,

'Dr. Sharvin, patient's flat-lined.'

Grace rushed to administer CPR without thinking about using the defibrillator. She pounded the patient's chest, hoping, praying she could kick-start his heart.

'Dr. Sharvin, he's gone, you have to stop.' Andrew's voice was soft and gentle.

Grace struggled to accept that saving lives was not always within her grasp.

Close to tears, she walked away to her office, shut the door, sat down and gave vent to a tsunami of emotions. Life was fragile, it was too much to have two deaths in ER in a fortnight, the life snatched from an unborn child in a reckless moment, and now, tonight, a man in the prime of his life, dead after an argument. In this moment she felt the loss of her mother, taken by the recklessness of an inconsiderate speed maniac, all her griefs collided in a confused collage of thoughts. She had to pull herself together to make rational decisions, the night was still young.

*   *   *

Life was a trek from one hospital to the next.

Grace walked into Mrs. Beresford's private room; she was having a bed bath, she waited in the corridor, pulled out her mobile phone and noticed an unsettling text message from Patience.

> *Hoping you are well Grace. I need to talk to you. May I come over tonight if you're not too tired? Let me know as soon as you can please.' Patience xx*

She replied instantly, letting Patience know she was welcome to come over. Grace feared her sister was in trouble — she was the tough one, always the happy one who got by with little or no complaints, the message spelled hidden desperation.

Grace chatted with Mrs. Beresford, struggling to keep her attention focused on the old lady's rambling.

'Will you come over again tonight, Grace?'

Grace found it difficult not to give in to the requests of others but had to be there for Patience that night.

'Here are some books and magazines I picked from the newsagency in our building, they send their regards and best wishes to you. These should occupy you today. I have to attend a meeting tonight but will come in bright and early tomorrow to see you. Is there anything you would like me to bring in for you?'

'Oh, you work too hard Grace, you must relax a little. Patience came in last night, she's arranging a carer for me when I get out of here. She spoke to my daughter in Alberta but they can't come out now, you know work pressures and that.' Her sadness was palpable. Grace had to extract herself from feeling guilty about not coming back later that evening.

*   *   *

Patience arrived laden with food as usual.

'Hi Grace, dinner's on me tonight, we are both going to relax and connect with what's going on in our worlds.'

'Dinner's always on you, even when I'm supposed to be cooking! It's too late to change you, you are Varuna's daughter. Without discrediting Mama Elsie, we cannot deny that Varuna enjoyed feeding people, hence the weight we both carry as proof of the pudding or should I say proof of the puddings we've eaten!'

They had a hearty laugh.

'You are skinny Grace, so don't say 'we', it's me that's the baby elephant! Mama Varuna always cooked like a famine was on the horizon and the children needed fattening to see them through leaner times! I don't know how she did it, cooking many dishes before I was up in the morning and she looked energetic with her usual, *carpe' diem* greeting.'

'Yeah, mum had a zest for life, like no other. Dear god, I miss her so much Patience.'

'I do too, Grace, but we are stronger for being raised by phenomenal women.'

They sat at the kitchen counter eating their dinner with Patience examining and savouring each morsel, the more chilli, the greater her delight.

'What's up at work Patience, you've had me in a frenzy today after I received your text message, what's up, girl?'

'Long story, we've both been so busy I had no time to fill you in on anything that has happened.'

'I'm sorry, I have no excuse for neglecting you too.'

'Remember I mentioned a few weeks ago that I received a call from an irate husband about his wife being removed from the marital home?'

'Yes, that was scary, what's happened since that call.'

'He is stalking me, last night I received a private Facebook message, here look at it.'

Grace put on her reading glasses,

I saw you take the garbage out now. Where is she, bitch?

Grace felt her skin prickle. She broke out in a cold sweat.

'This is serious, he is watching you which means he intends to harm you. What did the police say after the last threat?'

'I must admit I am a little shaken by this message. The police said they could not act on a nebulous telephone call, they needed something more substantial before they could list this as a case and assign someone to it. The darn cheek of the policewoman, she asked if I was in a relationship with the caller. She did not listen to a word I said about the situation.'

'It might be time to get Felicity involved to exert her influence in getting attention on this. He is upset and dangerous which puts your safety at risk.'

'Felicity does not know about this, I have reservations about telling her, she will overreact and then assign a bodyguard to watch over me. She means well, but she… she can become over-whelming, you know.'

'I get what you're saying but that might be what you need, a bodyguard, for your safety.'

'Oh Grace, please don't you go soft on me now, he will simmer down. His wife does not want to return to him, you know how some women become attached by the umbilical cord to abusive men. Not this one, she wants to carve her own life, free of her controlling husband. I think our motivational classes have influenced her. Good on her for that!'

'You need to spare a thought for *your* safety too. Let's call the police now and get someone over to alert them to your Facebook message, it's a veiled threat, telling you he's close by and by implication may attack you.'

'Let's not get too carried away, I'll do that tomorrow, I'll go down to the police department on my way to work.'

'If you think you'll have Felicity hot on your tail, be prepared that I will be keeping tabs on you too!'

'You both are nightmares!' she laughed, 'with the situation I was in when the chief's people took me, it was more the devil I knew, this time it's someone I have no inkling about, other than his violent behaviour towards his wife because of his insane jealousy and paranoia.'

'He is dangerous and it's foolish to sweep it under a rug.'

'I will attend to it in the morning, I promise. Now tell me, how are your sessions with Dr. Deakin? Is there a breakthrough yet?'

'It's going well, thanks. Nothing major to report just yet. Oh, I forgot to mention earlier, I'm meeting Virginia Bale for coffee in the morning. She asked to meet.'

Grace shut down when her personal life was in danger of being exposed. She felt guilty for shutting Patience off when she was open and honest about her life.

She shifted the conversation from Virginia Bale to the latest book she was reading. Her soul was exclusive, she was not ready to let anyone in to her hidden secrets, not even Patience.

22

Women in Distress

It was a crisp, cloudy morning, Grace was elated; a gentle breeze blew through her loosely hanging, soft curly hair. She was meeting Virginia Bale at *Coffee House* in Summer Hill that morning. Virginia waited outside the coffee shop, they had met once and might not recognise each other after that hellish night in ER.

A young, gaunt woman, paced the pavement at the entrance, cigarette in hand, puffing in rapid succession.

'Virginia?' Grace asked in her customary soft voice.

'Oh hi… good morning Dr. Sharvin? Sorry about the smoke, I'll put this out now.' She waved her arms about trying to disperse the cloud of smoke around her. Virginia looked no older than eighteen. Her dull hair was thin and wispy. The freckles on her face gave her a child-like look. Her eyes struck Grace as one who had life experience beyond her years, with the weight of the world on her stooped shoulders.

'Let's go in, I haven't had my coffee this morning so I might be a tad feral,' Grace joked, attempting to put Virginia at ease. She looked disconcerted, unsure how to react. Her subdued manner and edginess were unlike the confident email Grace received.

Grace who struggled in new social situations felt the need to reach out to Virginia, an unknown, unsure ghost.

They ordered coffee and toasted ham and cheese croissants. Virginia wolfed down the piping hot coffee and croissant.

'May I get you something else, Virginia?'

'Er… no… sorry for gobbling that down, I haven't eaten much these past few days.' Her unashamed declaration confirmed Grace's belief that she was struggling to survive on so many levels.

'Was there a particular reason you wanted to meet me today, Virginia?'

'Yes, to say thanks for the night I came to ER and for setting up my care with Patience. She is amazing.'

'No need to thank me, I was doing my job. You had so much to deal with that night, and I too wanted to know how you were getting on after you went home. Patience is the most selfless person I know.'

'You were more than doing your job, Dr. Sharvin, your gentle, kind way, is something I've never felt before.' Grace listened, taken aback with the comfortable way in which Virginia addressed her, almost as though she had known her for a long time.

'That's kind of you to say so, Virginia. Tell me how things are going for you now.'

'I am much better, losing the baby was God's choice for me, I think. Larry, my boyfriend would not have been a good father. I stayed on with him because I had nowhere to go. My grandmother is ill and could not cope with another mouth to feed if I had the baby, where would I have gone?'

'Was Larry abusive throughout your relationship? How long have you known him?'

'I'm twenty-four this year, we were dating on and off since I was eighteen. Whenever things got bad I moved back to my grandmother and when Larry begged me to return I did. The relationship got worse when I got pregnant. He became more aggressive and you know the rest.' She stopped, not wanting to relive the details of this torrid time.

'You are twenty-four, you have your whole life ahead of you. Losing a baby is difficult and you will be experiencing the physical effects of giving birth, reminding you of your loss. This is my concern for you.'

'The truth is I wondered if you would meet me today, I wasn't sure, but after what you did for me, your gentle way and your concerned call, made me want to talk to you again. Do you have children, Dr. Sharvin?'

Grace felt awkward for a fleeting moment before she answered, 'no, I don't have children, I never married.' She realised that she had to rephrase what she had just said. 'What I mean is that I never met the right person, my friends tell me I'm married to my job.' Grace smiled as she revealed part of her personal self to someone she was meeting on a social level, for the first time.

Virginia frowned, she did not understand how someone could give their lives to their job or show such kindness if they did not have children themselves. She could not find words to say what she thought.

'What are your plans from this point onwards Virginia?'

'Patience is arranging a job for me at the florist near my grandmother's home. I want to also help Patience with the safe houses for women but she says I need to get a job to take care of my grandmother first and consider assisting later down the track.'

'It sounds like Patience has it all mapped out for you. Heed her advice, you are in good hands.'

Virginia's traumatic ordeal was already behind her as she planned her next step in life. She said her grandmother raised her from the age of three when her alcoholic mother disappeared. Her father moved to New York to be with a woman he met on a dating site. Beneath the struggles, Virginia had an admirable, quiet resilience.

They parted with the promise to keep in touch. Virginia walked up to her, and gave her a tobacco laced hug, catching Grace by surprise.

The sun peered through diminishing clouds, the gentle early morning breeze had eased. Warmth trickled into her world.

*   *   *

Grace wanted to know what the police had put in place to ensure Patience's safety.

'Well, well, well, this is what they had to say, I am to delete my social media profiles until the situation *dies down*. Nothing else, and to add insult to injury, I am apparently courting trouble by advertising my campaign to assist women in distress. Helping others appears to be frowned upon by the police. I cannot shut down my social media profiles. How will women in distress reach me? I'm better off increasing my security around the house and maybe, if I had the time, I would take on a self-defense class!'

'Oh Patience, this is terrible. The last message was a pointed threat. Please allow me to hire protection for you, we have to act on this right away.'

Patience heard the anxiety in Grace's usually soft, controlled voice. Deep down, she knew, the threats could become dangerous and should not be ignored.

'I'll arrange it Grace, I'll talk to Felicity today for suggestions. If I need you to step in, you know I will ask you first.'

'You seem to be dragging your heels on this and that worries me. At the risk of sounding like a doomsayer, you know the situation might get worse.'

'I am serious about my safety, so I will act on this today.'

'I'm glad to hear you are being serious for your own sake, for once. Keep me informed of the outcome. I met a nervous Virginia today, but she warmed up as we chatted. Looking at her life, made me think I should not complain about my mine. She's had it tough for one so young.'

'Poor girl, she got involved with the wrong guy and her life deviated from what could have been a better life. It's not too late, she's an intelligent young woman, she has to make a living now, to feed herself and support her grandmother, and think about studying. She has a sense of pride, I've never seen before from one in her situation, she won't accept social support. It's good she has a job now. She's keen to be a social worker too.'

'She's excited about the job you arranged for her.'

'It's a temporary position until she finds her feet again. I'll call you tomorrow, I need to chat to Felicity.'

Grace prepared a light early dinner of grilled fish fillets and a green tossed salad before she headed out to see Mrs. Beresford. A few hours of sleep was wishful thinking, she had a lot to add to her conference paper.

The song she selected from Dr. Deakin's playlist was slow enough to make her drowsy, with no triggers into her locked memories. She contemplated asking Virginia if she could include her as a case study in her paper on the emotional trauma of abuse. Patience would have to approve this before she approached Virginia.

The late afternoon news was abuzz regarding a male

celebrity's harassment of female colleagues — this struck a chord on the vulnerability of women since the dawn of time and her own experience with the infernal Dr. Raja in South Africa. The twenty-first century was nowhere near eliminating these heinous crimes. Grace recalled the time of Patience's kidnapping and the stress it put the family through. Her mother bore most of the pressure in trying to find Patience. It was a dire problem that affected the blood, skin, and heart of her family. Grace admired Patience's service to women, catalysed by her own dark past. Her simple lifestyle, humble earnings for her community service, and refusal to accept personal financial assistance from Grace was praiseworthy, in a time of escalating living costs. Her commitment to the re-housing of women in distress depended on the generosity of affluent others who shared her sense of social justice. They served others, as did Felicity, and yet their personal worlds, while rich in their sisterhood, was empty without the adoration of a life partner.

Grace pulled out her journal from the bottom of her desk draw. She wrote in it for the first time since her mother's death.

What is life without love, what is love without light?

23

Called to Care

The events in Patience's world required the summoning of physical and emotional energy from Grace's daily, depleting tank of demanding schedules and pervasive dreams. She had to keep abreast with Patience's protection from maniac husbands who found her *Sisters Helping Sisters Organisation* a threat.

It was a scorching forty degrees, burning sidewalks, melting tarmac, wilting trees weather. Grace walked with a slower step, languishing in the warm evening air that hung low, promising a fretful sleep for those who worked daylight hours. The heat had escalated too soon this summer, inviting bush fires to unsettle the holiday season.

She mulled over the beauty of the Australian landscape, heat, and damaging fires, the resilience of the people who picked up and rebuilt on the land they loved.

Virginia Bale had the same unstinting resilience — this baffled Grace.

The Black Saturday fires were devastating. Her mother sat glued to the television, distraught that families had lost precious photographs, beloved pets, and prized livestock. Her mother donated whatever she could to the fire charities, to do her bit. She loved Australia and was grateful for her family's safety and the good people she befriended. She coerced Patience, Felicity, Mrs. Beresford and Grace to make substantial contributions to assist fire ravaged families. Varuna felt the pain and struggle of others as her own. Deep down she knew her mother had had a profound impact on Patience's choice to be a social worker.

Andrew Lang was not at work that evening. Nobody seemed to know why. He was always punctual and never missed a rostered night. Grace contemplated calling him and decided not to when she found an email she had missed earlier in the day explaining that he had picked up a gastro bug. Grace picked up the office telephone and dialled Andrew's home.

'Hi, Andrew, sorry that you're unwell. Are you keeping up your hydration?'

'Hi Grace, lovely of you to call, I could use some pre-mixed electrolytes but my own mix will have to suffice until I can get out the house again. I don't have a range of meds at home — poor doctor — I can hear you thinking!'

She heard a smile in those words and appreciated that he was not seeking sympathy, she had heard countless women complain about ailing men turning into attention seeking babies.

'I'll send someone over to you, the paramedic team will be on the road soon, cruising around hot spots in the event of an emergency. They could stop over at your place with a pack. Is there anything else you need Andrew?'

'Thank you so much, only if it's not too much trouble, I need to restore my energy. As for me needing anything else, well yes, if it were possible, your company Dr. Sharvin would be welcomed.' Grace did not respond to the last comment, unsure whether Andrew was joking or flirting.

'I hope it's not a busy night in ER, Grace, I feel awful about being away.'

'Thank you, sir, I would prefer you being at home with the gastro which appears to be severe. I don't need a doctor casualty tonight!'

'Ouch, even as a joke that's unkind coming from you.' Andrew's faint laugh convinced her, he knew she meant well.

'You should receive the electrolytes in an hour, get some rest now and more fluids down.'

Grace ordered a basket of fruit from the all night store downstairs in the hospital building, packed up a box of electrolytes and sent it off to the paramedic crew.

'This for the 'pretty boy' then, Dr. Sharvin,' the youngest male paramedic said. Grace cringed, hoped that the fruit basket had not created suspicions about her apparent 'liaison' with Andrew.

'He is quite ill and has no assistance so the team here has pitched in to help him on the road to recovery.' Her ears burned as she uttered a defensive white lie.

The twinkle in the young paramedic's eye annoyed her, his, 'yeah, I'll bet, it pays to be a 'pretty boy' around here,' made her bite her tongue to avoid any further speculations about Andrew and worst of all her predilection for 'pretty boys'. She had a heightened sensitivity to any criticism that suggested she was unprofessional or immoral.

It was going to be a lonely night in ER without her right-hand doctor. He was professional and dedicated even though his occasional banter unravelled her at the best of times.

The night was uneventful apart from an ice addict who was brought in after he was found wandering around city streets, proclaiming he was Adolf Hitler, talking to his imaginary followers, ready to lash out at anyone who questioned his intentions for a pure state. He grew increasingly agitated, creating a ruckus which unsettled patients who were waiting for medical attention.

Grace sedated him and had him put into separate high care, to sleep off his grandiose hallucinations.

*   *   *

All Grace could manage was a quick visit to Mrs. Beresford that morning. She grabbed another basket of fruit on her way out of ER. The most delectable mangoes, lychees, and persimmons were at their best for the season. Mrs. Beresford was not in her room, she was having a few tests that morning. Mildly irritated that she was not informed, Grace accepted she had no right to expect communication from the hospital on such matters, she was not next of kin. She wrote a cheery, hurried note, placed the fruit basket on top of it and left.

She stopped at the coffee shop for a quick breakfast, a dash home for a shower and then an early appointment with Dr. Deakin. She made a mental note to call Patience before she had a nap later in the day.

Dr. Deakin complained about the heat and awful muggy night, after a few minutes of casual chit-chat they settled down to business.

'Have you had any connections to the music on the playlist?'

'No, nothing yet although I had the dream which seems to be progressing — no longer someone walking past me, it was terrifying... I was trapped in the car and the hooded figure prised the door open and got into the car. I woke up at that point to the blaring sound of my alarm clock.'

'This is a significant shift, before I proceed, did you listen to the same song again?'

'No, I tried the next one on the list which ended up being a lullaby!' Grace laughed. Dr. Deakin noted the change in her mood.

'I'm going to put you under hypnosis, are you comfortable with me doing that?'

'What do you hope to achieve with that?'

Dr. Deakin was thrown by the sudden abruptness in Grace's attitude.

'It's necessary to jolt the next part of your memory, Grace, now that there seems to be an advancement in your dream recall.'

'Yes, I understand, but please, if I'm stressed during the hypnosis, will you stop?'

'Absolutely, your wellbeing is my priority, I will halt the process if your body language signals distress.'

'I do trust you, it's just that I don't want to be audible to your other patients in the waiting room.'

'Nobody is due in until ten o'clock. My receptionist will only be in around that time, she never comes in earlier. Does that make you feel better?'

'Yes please, go ahead.'

'Close your eyes and listen to my voice, you are tired, very tired, your arms are heavy, your legs are light, you are falling, falling, falling...'

Within seconds, Grace slumped over with a heavy sigh. Dr. Deakin continued.

'You are in the car, who is the person that got into your car?'

I can't see his face, his hood is floppy; it conceals the shape of his face... I see his eyes, they look like they are on fire, bright and large, they are... Grace halted, her breathing quickened, her voice raised with palpitating anxiety,

I have to find my phone, I have to get out; I have to get out...

'Why are you afraid Grace, what about this person makes you afraid?'

Grace shook her head, *I know he wants to hurt me, I know, I know... please, nooooo!*

Dr. Deakin snapped her fingers, 'you are awake Grace, you are awake; you are safe; you are here in my office; hush now, be still, take a deep breath.'

Grace opened her eyes, looking around the room, searching for confirmation that she was in a safe place.

'How are you feeling Grace?'

'Tired, so tired, I need to sleep... I must leave...'

'I want you to stay where you are for at least ten minutes before I can let you go. I need you fully alert now. What am I holding up in front of you?'

She struggled to focus as the book Dr. Deakin was holding up swam into her view.

'A book, the one you had on your desk when I walked in.'

'Good, you're back. Can you recall what you said?'

'Yes, I was afraid of the person, I could not see his face, his eyes were unusual; they were bright, so bright and large, but his face, there is something familiar about his face.'

'That's good, your memory is quite strong, I want you to focus on the face, we have to figure out who he is to understand what happened.'

'I want you to continue going through the playlist just before you sleep. Will you leave a voice recorder on while you are listening to the music, please don't turn it off, even if you are falling asleep.'

'Yes, I could do that, should I call you if I have a new recollection?'

'I would like you to. If I'm in a session or meeting please email me your thoughts before you do anything else in your day. A quick email with just the core memories that surface. We need to understand the source of your anxiety soon. I want you to go to Amsterdam without this anxiety to allow you to enjoy new experiences.'

'Is it possible to achieve this, so soon?'

'Yes, with what I've detailed to you, I'm confident we are close to a breakthrough, Grace.'

'Thank you. I will call you if I feel anxious after this.' See you next week.'

'Yes, do that, try to relax a bit more during the week.'

Grace walked out onto the street, she knew the memory relived today would linger.

24

Friends

Felicity arrived on the first flight into Sydney that morning. Grace stayed over with Patience after the situation that arose that night.

She often urged Patience to move into an apartment which she refused to do. She found apartment living claustrophobic and enjoyed having her own garden where she could grow a few herbs and have a few chooks. In the early days of setting up her organisation to protect women, she opened up her home as a temporary shelter from abuse.

Felicity rushed to Patience, embraced her in a locked grip, not wanting to let her go. She asked several times, 'are you okay, did he hurt you?' and begged, 'please come with me to Melbourne for a week, you can work from there. I'm worried about you being on your own at night after this.'

Grace stood aside to allow Felicity to run through her

emotions, before she said, 'Patience can stay at my place. I'm there most of the time.'

'You work nights, this will have me in a frenzy, knowing Patience is on her own.'

'It's a secure block.' Grace felt her jaw tighten to an uncontrollable twitch. It was Felicity's way of wanting to control things her way or no way.

'Let Patience decide,' Grace said, turning to Patience.

'Ladies, I think you both are more stressed than I am, I'm fine to stay here, he is in custody now and I can't leave Sydney, I have a lot to arrange with the new intake of cases here. The sisters need my support, especially those who came in, in recent days, they need familiar faces around them.'

'What about your ordeal? You can't ignore that you had a horrific experience. When are you going to put yourself first? If you won't come with me to Melbourne, then please stay with Grace for a while, please Patience.'

'Let's leave that decision to after breakfast, we are all frazzled, a cup of coffee will clear our heads.'

Grace walked to the kitchen to avoid Felicity's straining at the reins attitude.

'I could rustle up scrambled eggs and mushroom on toast if you both don't mind a light breakfast.'

'I don't think I could stomach any food right now.' Patience said, touching her belly before Felicity piped in, 'coffee is most welcome though, thanks, Grace.'

The quizzical look Grace received from Felicity did not prepare her for what she heard next.

'How are things with you Grace? Have you been to see your therapist after your breakdown in Melbourne?'

With her own weight of the world, Patience had the common sense to defect the insensitive situation from turning sour, 'no, Grace has been too busy, and that was a once off situation. She needs grief counselling but has not booked a visit yet.'

'You should not put it off any longer Grace, you should have seen yourself that night. I intended videoing your performance on my phone for some self-analysis, but your sister here, would not have me do it.'

Grace summoned every ounce of self-control to curb the rising urge to argue with Felicity.

Patience butted in, 'you both don't know everything about what happened here last night. So, if you don't mind Felicity, let me fill you in.'

'Please go ahead, I didn't mean to underscore what happened here last night, you know my scatty thinking!' Felicity walked up to Patience, sat next to her and held her hand.

'I got home from work around seven o' clock last night and found my front door ajar. I thought Grace came by but knew she would have called before she did.'

Grace looked on with mounting fear, she knew Patience would not spare graphic details. She remembered feeling she was inside the chief's compound when Patience described her days there. Even as a child she created vivid stories, telling them like one narrating her memoir. She felt the muscles in her neck tighten, her pulse accelerated, she wrapped her hands around her coffee mug, listening, sitting on the edge of her seat, astounded that Patience was prepared to recount her ordeal so soon after the trauma.

Grace's unemotional exterior belied the fear that welled up inside her, obscuring her emotional fragility.

'I knew as soon as I entered the house, that it was not Grace. A strong smell of cigarette greeted me, a 'just dumped,' burnt smell and the nauseating odour of stale male perspiration was in the air.' Felicity let out a gasp, Patience nodded and continued,

'I called out, *who's in my house, please come out now, you can take whatever you want and leave, I won't call the cops if you leave now!*' My ankles locked, I could not move for a second but knew I could not let this intruder know I was quaking in my boots. I was worried that he might be armed.'

Grace closed her eyes and began swaying in her seat.

'Grace, are you exhausted? Should I continue?'

Grace sat upright, embarrassed she was perceived as losing her grip, 'please carry on, we need to know all the details.'

'From behind me, as I passed the hallway dresser, I felt a large, soft hand, flat across my mouth and I heard, *'shut up or I'll kill you!'* It was then I realised it was Kitty Crankshaw's husband, he was holding the blade edge of a knife against my throat. He kept saying, *where is she, who do you think you are, breaking up families?* I told him, Kitty would only be back if he proved, over a period of time, that he had mended his ways. That seemed to calm him because he wanted to know how long was 'a period of time."

An agitated Felicity struggled to remain quiet, she erupted, 'Patience, did he rape you?'

Silence commanded the room.

Patience halted mid-sentence, unable to respond. Grace rocked in her seat shaking her head in disbelief.

'No Felicity! He wanted his wife back that is why he was pursuing me.'

Grace raised her voice, 'Go on Patience!'

'What's wrong with you both, it's a legitimate question. My life in foster care taught me that when a man gets a woman alone, there's only one thing on his mind.'

'May I go on?' Patience growled.

'Yes, I apologise for butting in, this is close to my skin.'

Grace whispered under her breath, 'you're not the only one.'

'He agreed to sit down in the lounge room and ask me a few questions. God must have been watching over me with our mothers close behind because he left the knife on the dining room table. All he wanted was to know about the organisation that protects women, questioning why we removed women from their marital homes and general inane questions. He said he was following me every day, hoping I would lead him to Kitty.'

'I'm sorry, I'm impatient to know how you got him into police custody? Did he hand himself over?' Felicity's mind was ticking, her investigative skills were primed just as much as her stress levels were elevated in her concern for her friend.

'He was calmer during our conversation, so I asked to go to the lady's room, as I had just come in from work, he agreed much to my surprise — that was my moment to act, I sent a text message to the last police officer I laid a complaint with, he acted on it and two of them came to the house within ten minutes of receiving my message. He got agitated when I told him someone was at the door, that I would send them away. This is when the police burst in. He's not a criminal, just a distraught, out of control husband.'

'Don't be ridiculous! He stalks you for days, he watches you outside your house, he breaks in and threatens you with a knife and you say – he's not a criminal!

'I know Felicity, it might seem that way. He was reacting to the emotional separation, his power was taken from him – he has psychological issues, not criminal intent. He left without resisting when the police officer handcuffed him, I'm still shuddering from the disappointed look he gave me as they took him away. He must feel I tricked him and robbed him of the prize.'

Felicity rolled her eyes in disbelief declaring, 'I don't know how you can be sympathetic towards this man, it's beyond me!'

Grace was quiet, mulling over, reliving the details of Patience's recount.

'We should go out for breakfast, being out the house will be good, what do you think Grace?' Patience's suggestion left Grace in awe of her bold, positive attitude.

'That's a good idea. Let's go over to the harbour cafe, it's good to be near water.'

'You and your mumbo jumbo, Dr. Sharvin, I don't know where the clinician is sometimes with all your ideas and pent up emotions!'

Grace felt the sting for the second time that morning, she dismissed her personal issues with Felicity. She had to be there for Patience.

'I have to slip out a little later to check in on Mrs. Beresford. I didn't see her yesterday so I feel I should pop in today.'

'Will you spend the night here with us?' Patience asked, cautious that Grace was annoyed with Felicity.

'Yes, thanks, Patience, I will be back with your favourite dish for dinner.' Grace smiled, not wanting to disappoint Patience.

'Chicken curry!' Patience squealed, 'just what the good doctor ordered for my speedy recovery, while others need chicken soup, I need chillies to warm my soul!' she laughed.

The harbour was abuzz with tourists, the sun was out in all its glory, making it perfect for an outdoor breakfast. Tensions eased, as they sat in quiet contemplation, watching the world go by.

*   *   *

Grace got to the hospital at 3 o'clock that afternoon. She walked into the ward, the head nurse ushered her out onto the corridor.

'We've been calling you all morning.'

'I have my mobile phone, you could have called me on that number, I was away from home since last night, is Mrs. Beresford okay?'

'We only had your home number on our records, I'm sorry to advise that Mrs. Beresford passed on in the early hours of this morning.'

Grace shook her head, willing away the news she was receiving.

'How? Why?'

She developed a pulmonary embolism during the night, caused by her hip fractures. Will you notify her next of kin?'

'My sister has the contact details for her daughter in Alberta, I will call her tonight.'

'What a terrible situation, it's obvious, her children did not care for her. You're the neighbour, if I recall, you brought her to the hospital. She said you were more like a daughter to her. Can I get you a cup of tea, this must be a terrible shock to you.'

'Thank you, I will pass on your kind offer of tea, I have to get to my sister as soon as possible to make a call to Canada.'

Grace walked around the hospital grounds, confused and lost in thought on the uncertainty of life. Visions of what her mother would have done came to mind. She walked to her car, sat back in the seat and sobbed for all she had lost in her life, and that poor Mrs. Beresford lay dead for the better part of a day, waiting for someone to claim her – Grace understood the fear and pain of loneliness.

25

A Different Daughter

The call to Alberta, Canada was a shock to both Patience and Grace. Grace read and reread the email glaring up at her from her laptop screen,

It is with regret, I inform that I cannot arrange nor attend my mother's funeral. Please utilise funds available in her banking account for the funeral arrangements. She was a private person and would not want any pomp and ceremony. If you require additional funds, contact me with details to whom and where the deposit should be made.

Signed: *June Beresford De Vaal*
Member of Parliament
Alberta District, Canada

'My goodness, no time to attend her mother's funeral?'
'I know Grace, it seems shocking, but let me tell you there

are many daughters like her in the world, too preoccupied with their own selfish needs. Unbelievable!'

'I can't say much, not having my mum around in my life. Truth is I did not form a close bond with any of the hordes of foster mums I had.'

Grace felt a whack in the head and a tinge of guilt. She was being hard in her judgements of Felicity of late, forgetting her harsh childhood. Varuna and Elsie epitomised perfect mothers, they raised their daughters to stand on their own two feet with the embedded view that life did not owe them anything; they had to work for what they believed in and wanted in life without forgetting those who were less fortunate than themselves.

'Well, we have to arrange the funeral, a private one is best — I won't be asking her officious daughter for any funds to bury her mother. How does she expect us to have access to her mother's bank account – we are just the neighbours.' Grace felt more peeved with the situation than Patience did.

'I think we should donate whatever the old lady has to charity, if we have access to her bank account, seeing Ms. MP is *too busy* to lay her mother to rest,' Patience added.

'The hospital staff were good to her, I'm sure they will attend. The other neighbours around us, in the building, are private, corporate types, I won't bother letting them know,' Grace added.

'Strange how life has changed,' Felicity mused, 'neighbourhoods were friendly back in the day, times have changed for the worse.'

'Yeah, people 'own' too much and become fearful the next person will snatch what they have, too much material wealth has corrupted good, common sense human values.' Patience looked at life from a humble perspective. Her altruism was unmistakable to those whose lives she had touched.

'A sense of 'otherness' that has crept into society has also led to the isolation of the elderly who become fearful when the media represents multicultural Australia in a negative, criminal, terrorist light. The wheat and chaff syndrome creates deep divisions among people. What is class without compassion, that's one thing money can't buy.'

'Wow, Grace, you are becoming deep, mystic and poetic these days! I hear the sense in what you're saying.' Patience enjoyed these profound, lucid observations of life that Grace dropped whenever she was angry or sad.

'Lots of heavy stuff this time on my visit to Sydney, what is it, state of the nation, state of the country or state of the world? I think we need to think about finding good people as partners to help us push our mission forward for a better world.'

Patience agreed, but Grace remained silent on finding a partner.

Felicity left for Melbourne with the promise to call every night to check in on Patience.

Grace sighed with guilty relief when Felicity's flight left Sydney.

*   *   *

A quiet, dignified funeral at the local church with five people in attendance, was Mrs. Beresford's final farewell.

A few days earlier, Patience approached the priest in Grace's neighbourhood to ask if they could have the funeral at his church. He welcomed the idea, saying 'we are all one, under the roof of God; this congregation is a group of humble folk who will send Mrs. Beresford off in prayer to her eternal rest.'

June Beresford De Vaal, MP of Alberta, did not send a message, nor make further contact with Grace.

'Oh, sad to close another chapter on life. We did not spend as much time with Mrs. Beresford over the years as Mama Varuna did, but I don't know about you, I feel sad now, knowing Mrs. B's children were selfish beasts, and she never let on once that this was the situation in her life.'

'I feel saddened too, more so by her situation, rather than her passing, to be honest. She suffered the ingratitude of her children with stoic silence.'

'Yes, some don't feel a moral responsibility, I know we are the way we are because of our mothers. Mama Varuna influenced my thinking as a role model in selflessness, she cared so much for my mother and more so when she was ailing. She will remain my guardian angel.' Patience could not hold back her emotions, Mrs. Beresford's death left her feeling her own sense of loss. Too much had beset her in recent weeks, the ability to hold it all in around others was remarkable — today she mourned for days gone by.

'We should cherish our childhoods. Did I ever tell you the Sanskrit meaning behind mum's name?'

'No, what does it mean?'

'It is a name given to the god of natural and moral law, the god of water and the celestial ocean encompassing and surrounding the world.'

'That is as we know her, you say god so is it a masculine derivative?'

'*Varuna,* in the scriptures, is male, his consort was *Varuni.* I suspect that the apartheid government officials, typical of the time, misspelled mum's name. It was a rigmarole trying to change the spelling in those days, and the registration office did not care a jot about ethnic names. So many surnames were mixed up, parents' first names became children's last names. Mum bemoaned not being called *Varuni,* but I think it sounds just as lovely and has profound significance, she embodied universal humanity in love and compassion.'

'Absolutely! She spoke her mind in matters that did not sit well with her, in unwavering truth, and she loved with no conditions imposed, a big, bleeding heart for the angsts of the world, so I can see the 'celestial ocean' encircling all, and upholder of 'natural and moral law' without a doubt. I am so glad my name was not muddled up and that I am the proud bearer of the *Sharvin* family name.'

'Nobody can dispute we are sisters, sisters from different mothers but loving sisters, nurtured by two angelic mothers, we are! I'm glad we're taking time to reminisce.'

'Aren't you glad we are *Grace* and *Patience* like *Varuna* is to us and many others as profound as her name, such is the hope for us? You exude your name, you have saved many a heart-breaking situation with your equanimity. *Young and wise art thou, Ms. Patience Sharvin!*'

'Likewise Dr. Sharvin, you are the prayer in your name.'

Tears sprung to their eyes as they acknowledged each other. They suspended all activities that afternoon, basking in glorifying both their biological and spiritual mothers.

*   *   *

With so much happening, Grace felt guilty for not checking in on Andrew Lang.

'Grace, how are you? I didn't want to call you, I know how hectic things are.'

'I have no excuse for not picking up the phone to check if you needed anything, but after a narrow escape and a death, I was a little rushed off my feet.'

'Jeez, that's major! I put it down to work but this is serious.

Are you up to talking about it or would you like to catch up for a drink later? I'm well and have revisited the world.'

'Not sure I can promise coming out for a drink later and we are on shift tomorrow night. Would you prefer meeting for breakfast tomorrow morning? I can fill you in then.

'Good idea, where shall we meet?'

'I'm meeting a friend at eleven o' clock tomorrow morning, so the earlier the better, around eight thirty is good for me. *Devon Cafe*, in Surrey Hills?'

'Yes that sounds perfect, see you then. Take care. Thank you for calling, Grace.'

She felt loads better for checking in on Andrew. He was a loner. His family hailed from the UK, he left to study and live in Australia. He was not the gridiron bloke type that Grace kept her distance from. He had a feminine side which he shared with her. She felt the need for the ear of a good male friend.

She contemplated whether she should tell him she was having therapy. She had already told him she was seeing 'a friend' after their breakfast that morning. Grace knew deep down that her inability to reveal too much of herself was her Achilles heel to meeting her soul-mate. She tossed around how or why she was this way when her mother was an outgoing people person. Grace jotted down the question she had for Dr. Deakin on how to overcome this hindrance in her personality type.

She pulled out her notes for the conference and gave it a cursory look, shoved it aside and turned on her laptop to look up places of interest in Amsterdam to make a holiday of her time there. Grace had not had a holiday in three years, she decided to add another week to her time in Amsterdam. She had accrued extensive leave which gathered cobwebs, and she was more likely to get taxed to death or receive a miserable payout.

After an hour of arm chair traveling, her concentration was

difficult to tie down to academic thought. She turned on the television. A documentary on the violent crimes against women was on. It was a snapshot documentary of three countries. She watched, glued to the screen as women spoke of the things they endured at the hands of male partners they had known for many years, or managers and colleagues who used emotional blackmail as a coercive ploy. She sent Patience a message to alert her to the documentary. She was close to being affiliated with the United Nation's Women's Organisation.

The documentary reported brutal attacks against women, ranging from eighteen to seventy-five as perpetrated by close family members and associates. Grace grabbed her notepad off her coffee table and wrote all she thought would help bring more clarity to her own disturbed emotional space.

She was desperate to feel life, breathe it, take risks and find love.

26

Unexpected Revelation

Grace missed her last appointment with Dr. Deakin. She scheduled a longer session that morning.

Complications in recent days left her with no inclination to listen to any new items on her therapist's playlist.

She arrived in a comfortable pair of slacks, loose cotton blouse and a pair of leather pumps she purchased on a trip to Bali.

'Good morning Grace, good to see you?'

'Hello, Dr. Deakin. Sorry for my late cancellation of the last session.'

'Yes, you've had a lot on your plate with your neighbour's passing. Do you feel like talking about that first, and don't you think it's about time you dropped the formality and called me 'Roseanne'?'

'I like the formality while I'm in therapy, it makes me follow through as you request or I might want to bend the rules! Being a doctor does not make me immune to being human in what I can avoid, you know.' Grace's mischievous grin took years off her.

'Whatever makes you comfortable is fine by me. How is your sister doing?'

'Patience is a tough cookie, I wish I had her inner strength. It saddens me when we are enmeshed in our work lives, that it takes something as serious as death, to make us realise we must make the effort to be there, not only for each other but *with* each other too.'

'It's good you've come to that acceptance and understanding, Grace. You both, as I have gleaned through our sessions, are close and nothing should come in the way of precious relationships.'

'Mrs. Beresford's passing and her daughter's callous attitude led to some deep ponderings, good ponderings. I'm reflecting on my life, and feel compelled to clear the dust if I am to feel the sun again.'

Her confident manner was what Dr. Deakin had been waiting for. As much as therapeutic advice was essential, its success depended on her client's mindset, the willingness to recover.

Grace was ready to move on from the demons that held her back.

'Yes, it's often that an unexpected challenge brings new self-discoveries, forcing us to reassess what is important in life. How do you feel about hypnosis again today Grace?'

'I want to close the door to my past, so go ahead with it. I've neglected to listen to more songs from your playlist.'

'Perhaps today's session will yield more to move you forward, let's begin.'

Dr. Deakin lowered her voice, sat back in her chair, adopting a meditative pose, with her arms hanging down the sides of her chair.

'Take a long, deep breath Grace, close your eyes, make yourself comfortable in the chair and let your thoughts wander wherever it will take you.'

Within seconds, Grace's disposition altered, her face was taut, and her voice was that of a child as she cried out, first in almost incoherent utterances,

No, please no, don't do that, my mum will be upset, please don't...

Dr. Deakin, surprised by this new narrative emerging through a child's voice, continued to gently coerce Grace to go on, 'who is that with you Grace? What are you afraid of?'

Its Boetie from next door, he's pulling my hair, he's angry, he's so angry...

'How old is 'Boetie' Grace?'

He works in dad's wood yard, he didn't finish school, could not study...

'Are you at the wood yard, how old are you Grace?'

I went with mum to take dad's lunch to him. I'm six years old.

'Where are your parents Grace, why are you alone with 'Boetie'?'

There was an accident, a man got his hand caught in the saw machine, mum and dad rushed out to help.

'Was there anyone else in the office? Where are you now?'

Nobody else, I'm in the office, he worked in the office, I'm in the office; mum told me to wait there.

'Why do you call this person 'Boetie', is it his name?'

He lives next door, his sister calls him Boetie; she's my friend.

'Do you like 'Boetie' Grace, is he nice to you?'

No, I'm scared of him, he looks at me, always looking at me.

'What happened in the office while mum and dad went to help the injured man?'

Boetie grabbed my hair, pulled me, to come closer...

Her breathing was rapid, short deep bursts, her anxiety visible in her fear-gripped child-like expression. She shook her head, her arms mimicking shoving someone away.

'You must tell me what happened, Grace.'

He touched my face, rubbing it over and over again, he opened my hair tie... it snapped... nooo! Mum will be upset... stop...

'Grace what happened?'

The telephone, the telephone rang in dad's office, I ran out the office, I ran and hid in the shed behind the office.

'Why did you run to the shed and not to your mum and dad?'

Mum said to wait for her... mum said to wait...

She sobbed like a child caught between obedience and terror. Dr. Deakin let her sob before she broke her hypnotic state.

'Grace, wake up, your dream is over, wake up.'

Grace opened her eyes, unsure where she was, she felt her nose drip and reached for a tissue from the box on the coffee table.

'How are you feeling Grace, do you need a few more minutes before we continue?'

'I need to go to the lady's room.'

Grace returned, nose powdered and hair straightened.

'Are you comfortable Grace?'

'Yes, I am, I feel a little drained but can go on.'

'I'll slow it down, take as much time as you need to answer each question.'

'Thank you.'

'Do you remember what you said?'

'Yes, it's very vivid. It's something I've not thought about in a long time. I thought he would kill me. I was terrified, terrified I had done something wrong.'

'What happened after that, what did your parents say?'

'They found me in the shed and asked why I was there. I told them I wanted to be with them. My mother asked where my hair tie was and that was it, we never spoke about it again except for reminders to always follow instructions given for my safety.'

'You did not tell your mother that 'Boetie' scared you?'

'No, I did not want to get into any more trouble, and Boetie would kill me if I told my parents what he did.'

'This is an unexpected revelation, but no doubt the reason for your underlying anxiety.'

'I'm not sure why this memory surfaced but trust you can make sense of it. My intention was to conduct an extended session today but I am reluctant to go through the process again because I think this memory might block where we left off in the last session and that is the catalyst I need to work on for your complete healing.'

'If you are free on Friday, I could come then, my shift starts at seven o' clock, I can set aside the day, I really want to get this out of my system.'

'You should get yourself off the night shift on Friday, if possible.'

'I'll be okay, what time can you see me on Friday?'

Dr. Deakin's receptionist confirmed that a double session beginning at nine o' clock was available.

27

Recesses of Her Mind

Virginia Bale made tremendous improvements in her life, the owner of the florist had enough faith in her proven honesty and dedication that allowed her to take two months leave for a long awaited overseas holiday. She was left to run the flower shop and manage a staff of three. She was studying for a Diploma in Applied Social Science at her local TAFE while assisting Patience on her days off.

Grace knew Virginia was a young woman whose potential had been side-tracked by a deceptive man. She felt like a proud parent who had given her child the opportunity to redefine her life. These successes were welcomed with pride by Patience and Grace, it invigorated them to see women's lives turned around. Life's journey called for a tank of inner fortitude to weather personal storms while cradling others. In serving others they grew their own temples of strength.

Friday could not have come sooner for Grace. She was determined to lay her ghosts to rest. Dressed in soft, cotton pants and singlet, she left her hair loose about her shoulders. It was a steamy December day, she wanted to feel cool, comfortable and unrestricted. Every fibre of her being craved release from the incarcerated fear that had claimed her peace.

*   *   *

Dr. Deakin was dressed in track pants, t-shirt and a pair of black, beaded, ballet slippers; she welcomed Grace at the door. Grace noticed a dress and jacket hanging up at the back of the office and a pair of black stilettoes at the side of Dr. Deakin's desk. She was aware that her therapist made every effort to make her feel comfortable.

'Good to see you are wearing cool clothes. We need our energies today. Let's use the inner sanctum for this session.' She led the way to a room tucked at the back of the main building.

'This is mysterious, I had no idea this crypt existed, should I be nervous?' Grace asked with a smile in her voice.

'A bit of nervousness is to be expected but rest assured, there's nothing to fear.'

'I'm placing my life in your hands now, just as my patients place theirs in mine, so I'm ready when you are. Wow, I hope I don't nod off in this comfortable recliner!' Grace's garrulousness was a giveaway for excited nervousness.

'Sit back, raise your feet and listen to the soothing sounds of the waterfall. I want you to feel totally relaxed. Close your eyes. Breathe deeply. Drop your shoulders, relax your hips and ankles, loosen your wrists and flex your neck like a spring ball.'

Grace felt the tension seep through her toes as her back and neck became floppy.

Dr. Deakin lowered the volume of the melodious sounds of the gentle waterfall.

'I am going to count backwards from ten, if you feel any anxiety, raise your left arm and I'll bring you back.'

By the count of five, Grace was in a deep state of relaxation, by the count of one, her head rolled to the left, her eyes were shut and her breathing was deep and slow.

'Grace, you are in the car on this rainy night, tell me what happened when the intruder got into your car, you saw his fiery eyes, who is this person?'

Grace pursed her lips, her head turned to the right, her breathing quickened.

No, no don't do this, please...

'Focus on his face Grace, who is this?'

Grace threshed around in her seat, she yelped, groaned and cried. Dr. Deakin let her go through a gamut of emotions and waited for her response. Grace touched her face and yelped in pain.

He's hitting me so hard, he hit me on my face, on my head. My nose is bleeding...

She wiped her hands on her nose and mouth.

I can't scream, my voice is stuck in my throat, oh no, he's burning me with his cigarette lighter, no, no, please...

'Who is this Grace?' Dr. Deakin knew she had to push Grace to acknowledge the identity of her attacker if there was any hope of ending her anxiety attacks.

I feel so much pain, my legs hurt... my arms ache... he's yanking my hair to loosen it. I lifted my knee, it knocked the car horn, it went off; he cut me on the shoulder and pushed my legs down.

'Grace who is hurting you?'

In a faint voice, Dr. Deakin heard Grace say,

Why Boetie? Why Boetie?

'What did he say Grace?'

There's a flashlight, shining through the window, he jumped up and punched the man; he fell to the ground. Boetie ran off into the mist and darkness.

'What did you do after that?'

I could not move, I tried to pull myself up in the seat, I saw the man on the ground, I knew I had to get away from this place. I foraged on the floor for my phone, the glass was broken; the battery was dead. I looked for my car keys, they were gone; I got out the car, my handbag was on the ground, I limped to the service station to get to the pay phone. I called 10177 and told them about the injured man. I went into the service station toilet and washed my face. I walked to a motel that was three kilometres away. My legs were hurting. I booked myself in and stayed there for three days.

'Grace, did you call your family to come and get you?'

No, no I could not tell my mother what happened, I failed her; I was a disgrace.

Grace sobbed as she processed why she locked away this dark, terrible situation that resurfaced after her mother's tragic passing.

Dr. Deakin knew that she had to bring Grace back, enough was revealed for a psychological decoding of what had just happened.

'Wake up Grace, you are with me in my office, open your eyes, you've done very well today.'

Grace looked around with the searching eyes of a new born, seeing the light for the first time. Dr. Deakin's voice emanated from a hollow chamber, her faint echo was difficult to understand. Her vision cleared as everything floated into sharp focus again.

'How are you feeling Grace?'

'Tired and thirsty, I feel I've been running a long distance. My arms and legs feel heavy. What time is it?'

Dr. Deakin brought Grace a glass of water and told her to sit up to clear her head.

'It's 11:30 a.m. You've been here for two and a half hours. It's normal for you to feel quite exhausted after such a long, deep session. Do you remember what you said to me now, Grace?'

'Yes I do, it was Boetie, Boetie Arendse who attacked me. If the hospital security guard did not arrive, I think, he might have killed me.'

'Did you tell anyone about this night?'

'No, I locked myself away for two weeks in my apartment in Durban, my mother could not know what had happened. I was so afraid it would make her ill. I felt too ashamed to tell my sister, I was supposed to be the strong one; I was planning a new life here for us.'

'Did the police or emergency services contact you? They would have found your car abandoned in the carpark, right?'

'Nobody contacted me, I heard through the hospital staff that the security guard was attacked when he tried to stop a man attacking someone. I asked a towing service to collect my car, it was not there when they arrived and was never found. That's the South Africa I know, I don't know what it's like now, but that went unresolved which is what I preferred anyway.'

Dr. Deakin listened in shock that nobody was apprehended for this crime against an innocent young woman.

'What about you Grace, did you not think you had to ensure this *Boetie* was apprehended, should he have the urge to attack you or other women again?'

'That is something I carry every day in my guilt-laden heart, I was selfish in choosing not to delay or complicate our imminent departure from South Africa. It would have halted the process if I proceeded with laying a charge. I know I have to ensure I follow up on this, somehow, if I am to put this to rest.'

'I could work with our services here to track him through our institution in South Africa, is that acceptable to you?'

'It is but please don't let him find out where I live, please.'

Dr. Deakin looked at the woman in front of her, she had harboured this terror during her selfless service to others both as a daughter in her family and a doctor to the community. There was still work to be done before her ghosts were eliminated.

'You have remarkable inner strength, Grace. You bore this alone for so long.'

'I am struggling with accepting that I chose to keep this from my darling mother who I know would not have judged me. I intended to tell her at some point but each time I tried, I couldn't go through with it. Then her untimely death stole the purging I should have done, years ago.'

'Yes, that is why the trauma of your mum's passing ignited your blocked memory. I'm not sure how you will interpret this, seeing that I'm acting in a psychological capacity with you. I recommend, whatever your spiritual belief, that you turn to this to help you heal from the guilt of not telling your mother. You need to turn to whosoever you perceive as your higher power to make peace with that and that you are not a sullied person. I also recommend that you sit down and have a heart-to-heart with your sister about what you've kept hidden. She has never probed but silently stood by you, through it all. I believe your final healing will come from this.'

'Thank you so much for your candour, I will heed your advice.'

'Keep a record of your dreams, although I don't envision the terror resurfacing.'

'Thank you once again, I hope I will be able to continue with my work for the conference with a much clearer head.'

'I need more details on Boetie Arendse, to start my trace

on him in the hope that we can burn the pages of that awful chapter.'

Grace left Dr. Deakin's rooms drained of every ounce of energy. She crashed on the lounge room couch and fell into a deep, dreamless, fourteen hour sleep. She missed her shift for the first time in almost two decades.

28

Time to Slow Down

Grace was hot and sweaty, her neck ached from her dead sleep on the couch. A multitude of missed calls and text messages choked her mobile phone. She was horrified when she realised she had missed her shift.

It was 2 a.m., she knew Andrew was still on shift. She sent him a text message to let him know she was coming in. Her phone rang the minute she hit send.

'Grace, are you unwell? I was so worried when I could not reach you, it's so unlike you not to send word.'

She heard his genuine concern which she only ever felt from her mother and Patience.

'Oh Andrew, I'm so sorry to have dropped you in the deep end tonight.' She struggled as she knew she had to tell another white lie to explain her mysterious absence from work.

'I took some flu medication on an empty stomach and it knocked me out. I can be there in forty minutes, I'm so sorry.'

'Don't be silly, you cannot come out at this hour, things are very quiet this evening as you can see from my ten or so missed calls on your phone! I am so glad to hear your voice.'

'Are you sure? Is there anything you need to be managed from my end, I have access to the hospital portal; I could update some records for tonight.'

'You need to slow down, go back to bed, Grace, it's under control, my numerous calls were only out of concern for you, not to complain that you were not at work! Who's the boss?' Andrew had a knack for easing her tension.

'Thank you, Andrew. I was thinking… would you like to meet up for dinner tomorrow night? Only if you are free that is?'

Grace heard a deep sigh on the other end of the line.

'Grace, I would love to have dinner. Where would you like to dine?'

'You decide, Andrew, I'm not fussed, any place for a quiet chat would be good.'

'What about the South African restaurant in Brighton? It might be a bit of a drive for you, what do you say?'

'*Hurricanes*? We could meet there, does six o' clock suit you?

'I could pick you up, seeing that you are under the weather.'

'I'll be good to get there on my own, it's doubling your time on the road if you were to pick me up. I'll see you tomorrow evening then. Call me if any crisis arises in ER before sunup. Thanks for your kind concern tonight.'

'Take care, no need for thanks, see you tomorrow evening.'

Grace wanted to cook Andrew a South African meal, but knew she would be sending him the wrong signal. She hoped initiating the dinner invitation was not misinterpreted. The truth had to be revealed, she valued his friendship. She was tired of secrets and subversions.

She found a note on her kitchen counter from Patience.

I was worried when you did not respond to any of my messages. Hope you don't mind, I looked in on you and found you in a deep sleep and decided to let you be. I looked for Andrew Lang's telephone number in your phone book, to let him know you were not coming in. I left a message for the hospital reception when I could not find his number. Not sure how reliable leaving a message with the hospital is. Call me the minute you wake up. Patience xx

Her throat was dry and sore, she blended apples, oranges and a bit of ginger for a refreshing, hydrating drink. Since she was alert she decided to work on her forgotten conference paper.

Virginia Bale agreed to share her experience to be included as Grace's 'live' research on the mental torment of being in abusive relationships. She was aware, in time to come, Virginia would add value to Patience's *Women in Distress Campaign*.

*   *   *

Patience came over early that morning with breakfast, an assortment of bread rolls, Danish pastries, croissants and piping hot coffee.

'Grace, good to see you're back in the land of the living, I almost had a heart attack when I found you dead to the world, obviously asleep for several hours. I was so stressed, I had to feel your pulse; you were so still.'

Grace laughed, 'At least I know I'll be missed when I'm gone!'

'Did Dr. Deakin sedate you to put you into a sleeping beauty state?'

'I had a very long session with her, there are some things I have to tell you now. You have been so gracious in not probing into my sessions with her.'

'You do the same for me, we respect each other's privacy, and I am your sister for enough years to know when there are 'off limits' topics with you Ms. Gracie!'

'Thank you, Patience.'

Grace opened up on the outcome of her deep hypnosis.

'Boetie was a bit too quiet, odd fellow, I thought. His family moved away from the area and we lost track of them after that. Mama Varuna would have been able to tell us what happened to his family.'

'I would rather not know, to be honest, Dr. Deakin is doing the investigation or rather getting her contacts to look into it.'

'I wish you told us, Grace, you could have prevented so many years of silent torment.'

'I know, but I shelved it so far back that I thought I had obliterated it. Mum's passing shook me and the guilt I felt for not telling her came back to haunt me.'

'The human mind is complex in what is easily retrieved and trauma can be masked by clouding memory. Amazing human mind control and resilience that we should appreciate.'

'The session drained me. I feel much lighter now that the truth has been unlocked, but there's a bit more to work on, that is, on myself. I think when I overheard ER staff refer to me as the 'ice-maiden' they were perhaps justified.'

'Don't be ridiculous! You are far from that and think about which quarter of the ER staff that comment came from. Don't dwell on it Grace, onwards and upwards now!'

'Thanks, Patience. I feel happy you know what was inhibiting me, all these years. Tell me now, are you coming with me to Amsterdam next month? I'm hoping you had a change of heart on that.'

'It's not possible, if Virginia was fully trained, I could leave things in her hands and keep in touch online. I could ask Felicity to assist her, but I'm concerned that she might push Virginia too hard or expect too much from her too soon, you know what I mean?'

'Felicity is Felicity after all, but she means well. I did hope you would be able to come over, I'm taking an extra week after the conference as a part of my overdue leave, and I might lose those days if I don't take them soon.'

'Good on you! I'm happy you're taking time for yourself.'

'Andrew Lang is a reliable, good doctor. I'm going to suggest to the hospital board that he be made Assistant Head of ER.'

'Great! This will allow you to have more time off down the track. Maybe we can take a much needed break together, that cruise we dream about!'

'Sounds like a good plan worth bringing to life. By the way, I'm having dinner with Andrew tonight.' Grace studied Patience's reaction.

'Interesting, anything new I should know about, dear sister?'

'If you mean anything new on a romantic front, it's a categorical no! We are good mates and that's the way it shall remain.'

'Better hope he knows that Grace, he is in awe of you so don't break his heart.'

'I have been making that clear to him, but tonight will be a night of revelations, I think.'

*   *   *

Grace enjoyed a cool evening drive to Brighton, she donned a pale, cotton summer dress and flat sandals. Andrew was waiting outside *Hurricanes,* wearing his dashing white smile. He walked towards her with his characteristic saunter, she cast

199

aside her inhibitions and accepted his gentle hug and peck on the cheek.

'I'm so glad you look well, you needed the sleep; you look refreshed. Overwork is detrimental to one's wellbeing, Dr. Sharvin.'

'That and a whole lot of other things which I hope to enlighten you on as my dear friend.' She noticed his flushed face and knew she had to impress upon him without any 'ifs' and 'buts', that all she could offer was a good friendship.

'Last night was an uneventful one in ER, all up four patients, one broken arm, two kids in a minor domestic burn accident, trying some experiment and one false alarm from a woman who thought she was in labour. It was a bit of gas from her large meal of extra hot Mexican fried beans, salsa, and sour cream!'

They laughed at the idiosyncrasies of their world which gave Grace an inroad to explaining her absence from work that night.

'I might not have mentioned, I have been seeing a therapist for some old anxieties that surfaced in the past year or so. I thought I could cope with it but it got a little out of hand, and I needed professional help.'

'As long as you are on the mend, that's all that matters. Please do not feel you have to tell me anything that makes you uncomfortable.'

'Well you know *us medics*, right? We think we can solve our own medical issues. I'm on the mend but have a bit more to process.'

Grace explained, sparing Andrew intricate details of the scars left from her attack in South Africa, and how hypnosis had unlocked what she had concealed from herself and the world.

'That's a huge burden to carry alone. I wish you the very best in casting it all behind you now. Thank you for your honest sharing of your ordeal, and more so for trusting me.'

'You are a good friend, Andrew, I hope I will still be a friend when you meet the right woman and invite me to your wedding.' She smiled across the table at him.

'I don't think I'm anywhere near committing to a long term relationship yet, and like you, I treasure our friendship and would hope that we can always be there for each other, in good times and bad.'

Grace was on her guard at first when she heard him say those last words. It echoed with the hint of hope, a vow just waiting for *'till death do us part*. She had to add a dash of humour to the moment.

'Thought you were proposing there Andrew!' She laughed and was relieved to see Andrew saw the funniness of his comment.

'Freudian slip eh? But in all seriousness, the man in your life, whoever that may be, will be the luckiest man alive.'

'You are very good for my ego, kind sir, I think the same of you.'

'Now that drinks are down, do you want to try the ribs or the *boerewors*, a spiced sausage, considered a delicacy by locals in South Africa.

'I think ribs and *boerewors* are what I'll have.'

'No Andrew, the 'w' in *boerewors is said as a 'v' as in* 'boerrrevorrrs.'

'Oh, you South Africans and the rolling 'r's' and 'v' for 'w' sounds!'

'Enjoy the feast!'

A pleasant evening passed in light-hearted conversation leaving Grace happy that she was not leading Andrew up the garden path.

29

New Lease

A few days before Grace was due to depart for Amsterdam, she received a call from Dr. Deakin asking her to come in to her rooms on her way to her shift that night.

She felt the familiar nervous energy begin to rise. Her disturbing dreams had not resurfaced since her last extensive session with her therapist.

Dr. Deakin had a bottle of champagne on ice with two glasses and a broad smile ready for Grace.

'I have some news for you that might settle everything. Have a glass of champagne to celebrate the end of an ordeal.'

'I'm going on shift tonight, thank you, I can't have any alcohol. What news do you have?'

'My contact in South Africa got back to me this afternoon with news that Boetie Arendse died five years ago.'

'Do you have proof of this? How did he die?'

'Yes I do have proof, the name and records are a perfect match. He was involved in a drug heist and was shot during a police raid. He is recorded as having had a pauper's burial as nobody claimed him as next of kin.'

Grace sat with her head bowed, not knowing whether to pity the man that tormented her for most of her life or to celebrate that he no longer existed to torment her again.

'Grace, what are you feeling right now, how does this news sit with you?'

'I'm relieved that he can't harm me anymore but my head is a mess now with how fearful I was, always believing he would find me and be back to torment me. I have to rethink my world and have a lot of catching up to do. Sorry, I'm not being ungrateful for all that you've done. I am indebted to you… I am a little tentative about my new life.'

'I'm here to support you through that.'

'Thank you so much for everything. I leave soon for Amsterdam so the change might be good for me. I will be in touch, should my anxiety return.'

'What are you doing to alleviate the guilt you are carrying for not having told your mother about your struggles?'

'… I haven't quite acted on that yet, although I've told Patience everything and Andrew Lang a bit about what I've been going through. That's a breakthrough for me.' Grace's eyes shone with pride that had she crossed her demon infested waters by sharing her dilemma with those closest to her.

'Wonderful to hear this. The guilt you carried for withholding your terrible experience from your mother is what we can work on to end the chastisement of yourself. In your understanding you were protecting your mother from suffering your pain. It's time to accept and celebrate the beautiful soul within you, Grace, the nurturing soul that the world needs today. You will feel brand new once you come to terms with not telling your mother.'

Grace listened to this alien biographical sketch of who she was – this was far from how she saw herself.

'Seek whatever spiritual healing you need, I am here to validate your selfless being.'

She raised her head, looked at Dr. Deakin and spoke with heavy emotion, 'thank you… thank you… I have to learn to believe that, I suppose.'

'Small steps is the way, the worst, I believe is over.'

'I am planning on taking a yoga and meditation class. My extended trip to Amsterdam is for more 'me' time.'

'Glad to hear it. I'll let you go now, I know duty calls; I hope you have a quiet night.'

Grace left Dr. Deakin's office, feeling carefree and happy, the concrete source of her anxiety was exorcised.

Andrew Lang could not contain his admiring glance as Grace stepped in through the glass sliding doors. Her hair bobbed around her shoulders, there was a fresh glow on her face. She smiled with open warmth; for the first time, he noticed how her eyes crinkled to little slits with her unrestricted smile, a smile not many had seen.

'Good evening Grace, you look amazing, did you have a good day?'

'I sure did, Dr. Lang,' she teased, 'if you care to chat during the dinner break, I'll fill you in.'

'*Oooh*, this sounds intriguing, have you met the man of your dreams?'

'Oh nothing as exciting as that,' Grace said with a playful air that Andrew had come to enjoy.

'I shall have to contain my bursting curiosity until the dinner break then.'

'Yes Dr. Lang, duty calls, let's get to it!'

'Will do, Dr. Sharvin.' He remembered being cautious around her when he first arrived in her department. She was distant and only spoke when necessary. This change made her alluring, he shoved that thought aside, knowing he had no chance of ever winning her heart. He was happy with having her respectful friendship.

The night had a few busy moments and long slumps. Grace worked through the night with a lightness and ready smile. She was grateful no major traumas came in that night.

*   *   *

It was a busy two days leading up to her departure for Amsterdam. Nervous energy crept in, she knew she had to be vigilant to avoid small accidents around the house. She had to gear herself for cold weather although the first week would be spent indoors at the conference centre.

As the only medical delegate from Australia, she wondered if she had to be prepared to explain her background, not in the medical field but curiosity about her race and culture. She was peeved the most on that score whenever she was at conferences in Melbourne or Perth. The comment, 'for someone who was not born here, you don't have an accent,' infuriated her but she chose never to respond to it. She shed the baggage that pinned down her emotional world and now was the time to take a confident stride and own her place in the world.

The additional time in Amsterdam was what she looked forward to the most. With not too many tours booked, she intended to roam on a whim, acting on impulse on how she felt each day. She had to break the structured life she led, covering up flaws, shying away from the promise of new friendships. It felt like a rebirth, knowing she would never be afraid again.

Patience came over for a late evening visit.

'Are you set with everything now, conference notes, packing and sightseeing plans?'

'Almost there, conference notes can always be added to, up to the last hour, I say, and as for sightseeing, I booked two tours and will be a roving tourist on other days.'

'Good to see the carefree spirit of youth return to my sister!' Patience jumped up, hugging Grace in a tight embrace. She had missed the Grace who had shut herself off after their mother's passing.

'I'm floating around on a high since my last visit to Dr. Deakin, it's been like weeding a stubborn garden, clearing the decks for a new launch of myself, I need to sustain this.'

'You look happier and who knows now that the South African dark side of your life, no pun intended, is over, you might want to take a holiday there some time.'

'Perhaps, but it's not on my cards now, I have a bigger world to catch up with and I hope you will take some of those future trips with me.'

'It seems possible with Virginia Bale showing great promise, I would love to have her as my second in charge soon.'

'Great to hear that, we need to create that space in our lives. Fate brought Virginia into our lives although her entrance was an awful one. She is driven to change her life and is well on that road. What's new on the Perth safe house now?'

'I haven't mentioned this, but it opens next month although it's 'unofficially' operating with just two women in the shelter at the moment. Felicity arranged for a few businesses to finance a dinner evening as the opening of the house.'

'You must be over the moon. Your effort is commendable in getting this difficult one off the ground. How is Felicity?'

'Not sure, to be honest, she has been a little hard to reach.

When I do speak to her, she always seems to be rushing to something or the other. I know the detention centre issues have kept her busy. She probably needs some space too.'

'Nobody needs space from you, you are the most unobtrusive person I know.'

'Thanks, sis, I can say the same for you! We are, after all, our mothers' daughters!'

'Mum made sure we did not turn out like the toxic folk in her life. Mothers are teachers and students of life. To be able to look ahead and not behind at one's troubles, is a noble feat'

'Ditto!'

'I know I have a bit more growing up to do in that area.'

'We all do.'

' Dr. Deakin said something unusual, I mean 'unusual' outside her professional sphere, she told me to turn to what was my spiritual or religious 'to-go-to' place to make peace with myself for locking mum out of the terror I experienced.'

'You should consider that Grace, it would bring you inner peace. You will have time to contemplate how you want to express this. I will miss knowing you are close by in the next two weeks but know that this time away is what you need. Is Andrew still insistent on transporting you to the airport?'

'Yeah, the flight departure time suits his schedule, and he wants to help, so I agreed to take his *Uber* ride.' Grace giggled, winking as she said this.

'He is a good friend, and I'm pleased you let him in, he made sure you did!'

Patience spent what was left of the night in the room that was always ready for her, a comfortable bed and a cupboard of clothes for any unplanned stayover.

Varuna's daughters shared an enviable closeness.

30

Amsterdam

Good morning ladies and gentlemen. Welcome to Schiphol International. It's a crispy-cool morning in Amsterdam at just 2 degrees. I hope you've had a pleasant flight. Whatever you are getting up to in beautiful, historical Amsterdam, remember daylight is from eight-thirty to four-thirty, plan your days around this schedule to get maximum value for your visit. Take care, enjoy your stay and we hope to see you again on board KLM!

Grace woke to the soothing, chatty voice of the captain and blinding, bright, cabin lights. She intended to look over Amsterdam on the descent, sleep claimed her in the last ten hours of the flight. The seat next to her was vacant, she stretched out, using it as her office space and private boudoir, before wafting off into an undisturbed sleep.

A conference organiser was appointed to meet her at the airport and settle her in at her hotel before lunch, to brief her on the conference procedure. Evening drinks were planned to meet, greet and get to know fellow presenters. She searched the sea of eager faces waiting to collect loved ones after a long flight. A placard with large red letters bearing her name was waved in the crowd. A short, blonde-haired woman called out to her.

'Grace, welcome, how was your flight?'

'Thank you, you must be Nina Holstead. It was good, I slept, almost through the entirety of the flight.'

'At least you're rested then. You should put your jacket on, the air is fresh outdoors. We don't want you catching a cold now, after your Australian summer.'

Grace was booked at the *Renaissance Amsterdam Hotel*, an 18 km drive from the airport. It was noted for its conference space and facilities.

'I think you will quite enjoy the hotel for the week you are there, it's centrally located and the train station is close.'

'I'm looking forward to my stay, I booked a week at the same hotel after the conference to take in the sights and history of Amsterdam.'

'Is there any particular aspect of the history you are keen on?'

'My South African background is something that makes me eager to understand Dutch culture and lifestyle. The Dutch were among the first European settlers that arrived in South Africa. I think I'm going to be excited by the cuisine and language. You sound British Nina, am I right?'

'I studied in Britain, married a Brit but my ancestry is Dutch so I'm happy to suggest places you might enjoy. I have an Australian link, my maternal great-grandmother is Australian, according to family legend.'

'Thank you; that will be wonderful. You have an interesting family history, a memoir in the making I daresay.'

Nina laughed, 'I don't know about that, there might be skeletons in the family closet!'

Grace smiled and acknowledged that every family had a few bones rolling around the family closet.

They arrived at the *Renaissance,* Nina left Grace to settle in for a few hours before lunch.

Grace's ankles were heavy and stiff, she peeled away her socks to reveal swollen ankles. The twenty-one hour flight had caused fluid retention. She was prepared with her stash of natural, diuretics. Patience responded to her text message with a call. It was Sunday night in Australia.

'Hello, I didn't expect you to call so soon.'

'Just needed to hear your voice and to know that the flight was good and that your 'meet-and-greet' person was waiting for you.'

'It was a very pleasant flight, Nina Holstead seems lovely; she was waiting for me. We are having lunch together a little later. One thing though, my ankles are swollen.'

'Those 'cankles' never fail to flare up on a long distance trip, but you have your meds, I'm sure.'

'Yeah, they should return to normal by morning. There are drinks on tonight to meet the presenters from across the world. To be honest, I'm not looking forward to that.'

'You can't be anti-social on your first day there, just be your usual intelligent, charming self, and all will be well.' Patience upped the optimism fearing Grace might slip into her reclusive mood and be in for a hellish time.

'If only to please you, I will try to be more outgoing. I'll send you a message on how it goes. Thanks for the call.'

*   *   *

A light lunch at *Scossa* was enjoyable, Nina's laid back manner made Grace comfortable enough to relax her guard.

'Do you enjoy living in Amsterdam Nina? Although I think the answer is obvious.'

'I enjoyed being in Britain but was miserable when I was in boarding school, I missed my family, particularly my mother and sister. College days were good, I had a casual job, rented my own space and saw my mother and sister as often as possible. My husband loved Amsterdam so it worked out well that we married and moved back to my home city.'

'Do you have children?' Grace heard herself say this with sincere curiosity, something she avoided asking and being asked.

'Yes, love of my life, I have a two year old, Finn, he is an energetic bundle of sheer joy!' Grace smiled as Nina's face lit up and blushed with pride and love for her little boy.

'How do you cope with picking me up, meeting me for lunch, attending the drinks evening and then the week-long conference with events that go well into the night?'

'It's called *moeder,* I would not be able to sustain my professional life if it were not for my mother.' She put her hands together in praying gesture.

'Yes, what would we do without our *moeders?* That's the Afrikaans word for 'mother' too, you know.' Grace felt a tinge of nostalgia in this comment. Her mother would have flitted around like a proud, expectant grandmother before she set out for Amsterdam.

'How about you, are you married? Children...?' Nina shot a glance to Grace's left ring finger and stopped with the awkward realisation that she might have been hasty in asking those questions.

'Not married, married to my job, I'm afraid. I just never met the right person. Children? I would have loved to have children…' Grace listened to herself as deeply-embedded hopes and desires surfaced with no caution nor fear of being judged.

'There is a grand plan in this universe for us all. You must meet Finn, I will arrange to have you over at the house for dinner after the conference, if you can fit it in with your plans.'

'I would love to meet Finn, but you will be exhausted after the conference seeing that you are part of the hosting party too.'

'Well, I have taken three days leave after the conference. I run a medical clinic with two other doctors who are willing to fill in for me as I do when they need time out. It's a great arrangement in a collaborative team. How about you? Are you in private practice?'

'That's a dream situation you have there. I work nights at a busy ER facility that I head up. I am on call round the clock though. I love it, but somewhere down the track, private practice might be on the cards.'

Grace was grateful that her entry into Amsterdam in the first few hours was pleasant and friendly.

Drinks were scheduled for 7 p.m. in *2B Lounge Bar* on the basement level of the hotel. Some local and all international presenters were in attendance. Overseas guests were residents at the *Renaissance Hotel.*

Grace showered, donned a black pair of slacks to conceal her bulbous ankles and a trendy, short, grey leather jacket, a pair of hoop earrings and a thin gold necklace. She had to sus out the expectation of 'smart casual' dress here for the evening functions. The conference itself called for a strictly formal dress code. She carried black, grey, cream and caramel suits for the conference days.

She stepped into the bar, chilled jazz beats played softly in the background, and the delectable aroma of finger foods wafted up her nostrils. The retro ambience is not what she expected. Medical conferences had a stiff air about them, the pomp and snobbish aura of those events made her feel out of place. Tonight she felt aglow and excited. Nina's broad smile welcomed her. Her hair was swept up in a gold comb, she wore a red cocktail dress and matching open-toed shoes.

'You look amazing Grace, oops that sounds good too! I love your name.' Nina had downed a few cocktails and giggled at herself.

'Yes, my sister used to tease me when we were younger, singing *Amazing Grace* when I was in a foul mood! You look wonderful too in red. I might be a tad overdressed in anticipation of cold weather.'

'You are perfectly dressed for the place and weather. I'm so tired of winter that I decided to make it my own summer evening! I have to put on my gigantic overcoat before I leave here, and I'm likely to have frozen toes on the way home.' Grace admired her the devil-may-care attitude.

A brief informal welcome by the Chairman of the Medical Board was followed by a flurry of greetings, reunions for some and new introductions for others.

'Come let me introduce you to some of the presenters staying here at the *Renaissance*. We have France, Ireland, Switzerland, United States, Britain, Canada and from your neck of the woods, New Zealand too! There they are, you can see the 'foreigners' have already become acquainted!'

'Good evening everyone, this is Dr. Grace Sharvin from Australia, Grace, I will leave you to meet each one.'

Everybody gathered around Grace, asking questions about where she was based and how long she had been working in ER.

Dr. Keefe Daly from Ireland asked if he could get her a drink and returned with a delectable fruit cocktail. He was very keen to know more about Australia as he was planning on taking up a contract there in a few months. Amidst the chatter, they spoke of their working lives as the rest of the room melted into oblivion. Keefe Daly was fascinated that Grace was from South Africa and asked if he could hear more about her medical experience there. He planned at some stage in his career to take on a contract there too. Grace caught a glimpse of Nina walking towards her as the evening came to an end.

'How was your evening Grace, I wanted to give you the space to get to know everyone. I see you and Dr. Daly hit it off. He is a lovely man, it's his second attendance at this conference. As you know we host this conference once in five years. I know he'll be interested in your paper and stance on violence against women and the far-reaching effects of trauma.'

'Why is that?'

'I'll leave him to explain his interest. I will adjust the seating in the morning so that he gets to sit next to you, I had the New Zealand delegate next to you, you don't mind if I swap that; do you? The New Zealand delegate won't have a clue that we moved him!'

'Not at all, it will be good to chat further with Keefe tomorrow, although I suspect there won't be much time for that with a host of presentations and the Q an A after each session. Poor unsuspecting Kiwi! Thank you so much for taking such good care of my needs today. See you in the morning.'

One cocktail down, invigorating conversation and good music, made Grace wish for the hurrying in of the next day.

31

New Friends

Grace received a barrage of compliments on her paper. Of particular interest to her audience was her case study on Virginia Bale. The ability to overcome such brutal abuse at the hands of a lover, lose a child, live in poverty and have the passion to help others, elicited questions on the subject's support network. Grace indicated that as doctors they had to have a network of support agencies available if they were to act as the bridge for the mental and emotional survival of their patients who were victims of brutal abuse.

Keefe was keen to have Grace come over to Ireland to present her paper there to trainee doctors who were in a prime position to form partnerships to improve outcomes for their patients. Nina sat next to Grace at lunch, she cozied in for a private chat.

'How are things going with Keefe? You should stay in touch with him once the conference is over.'

'He's been lovely, yes we might choose to remain in touch with each other. Nina, are you on some agenda here that I'm not aware of?'

'Well, Keefe did say he was so impressed with your work. Thing is he asked if I knew if you were attached?'

''Attached' as in a husband or partner? What did you say?'

'Just that you were married to your job and otherwise free as a bird and ready to be ensnared!' She nudged Grace, almost knocking the wine glass out of her hand, laughing at her attempt at matchmaking.

'Nina, now that is going to make me very awkward around him, we've been engaged in professional conversations.'

'Grace, I know we barely know each other, but you should see yourself when you talk to him, you glow in his company, and he can't take his eyes off you even when you are across the room from him. Professional conversations can be romantic, you know!'

'I think you are willing this Nina. So, are you acting on his behalf or mine because nobody can deny your Cupid's bow and arrow are out for a killing?' Grace giggled. The bond between them formed quickly in that week giving license to discussions on matters of the heart. 'What about him, a man his age must be in a relationship?'

'I knew it! You are interested. He's been divorced for five years now, no children, it was a brief marriage, it ended three months after the nuptials. And on the subject of whose behalf I'm working on, well... it's on behalf of two beating hearts who are too shy to take the next step!'

'How do you know all this? I barely know the man Nina and I am a tad 'shy' by nature.'

'I got to know Keefe quite well during his last attendance at the Amsterdam Medical Conference, five years ago. I introduced him to my husband who is a pathologist. They have been friends ever since. What do you say to me having you both over for dinner before you head back to Australia?'

'I'll let you know once my touring plans are satisfied. I want to get in as much as I can of Amsterdam, I don't know when I'll be back.'

'You'll be back, everybody returns! I'll call you later next week to confirm. Keefe's walking this way, I will leave you two to get further acquainted.'

Grace spent a pleasant afternoon at the conference. Now that her presentation was over, she was relaxed and open to noticing the kind, blue eyes and good crop of soft, auburn hair on Keefe's head. He was a tall man, almost six foot which made Grace's lack of height noticeable. He was an attentive man, a great listener, and conversationalist. She found him intriguing enough to toy with the idea of accepting the dinner invitation, Nina extended.

She had to get Patience's opinion on this situation.

'Hi, Patience. I hope my call did not disturb your beauty sleep. I have something interesting to tell you. How have things been?'

'Oh, Grace I'm so glad you called, I'm devastated!'

'What's happened?'

'Please tell me about the conference before I go on my rant.'

'That can wait, nothing out of the ordinary to other conferences I've attended. Tell me, what's happened.'

'You know I've been complaining that Felicity has been scarce lately, avoiding contact with no explanations.'

'Everybody needs their space at some time, don't take it personally.'

'How can I *not* take it personally, you would too if you knew this. I hope you're sitting down.'

'My goodness, this sounds serious, are you unwell?'

'I am furious, anything but unwell! Felicity called yesterday, after several weeks of saying she was too busy to chat, to tell me she married the retired journalist, Alf Refalo, at the court house in Melbourne. I had no idea she was even dating someone. Is that what a friend does?'

'Refalo? He's got one foot in the grave! What was she thinking?'

'Why would she not tell me, Grace? I am so disappointed that I was not trusted enough to be told!'

'She probably thought you wouldn't approve so she did the deed and then told you. What does it matter?'

'I am hurt Grace, why would I discourage her if she loves him. Unlike you, I have nothing against age in relationships. Do people do this to their close friends? I don't know, I don't have many to know. It's a significant, happy decision in her life and I was excluded from knowing about her joy in love. Now she wants us to come to a reception dinner she's planning at the end of the month.'

Grace had never heard Patience explode this way, her anger and hurt were at full throttle.

'Let it go, she will probably explain why she rushed into this. Just be happy for her. I understand that you are questioning the relationship she has with you. She can be impulsive at times so who knows how this marriage came to pass.'

'Right now, I want to wallow in my disappointment, but I suppose, you're right, I should forgive her… her happiness matters to me. I will try to move past this moment. I don't intend to lose the friendship over this, I'm just really upset right now. I'm beginning to get frustrated that I have to always be the forgiving and tolerant one in my friendship with Felicity.'

'Your namesake says it all. It's a friendship worth hanging onto, Patience. I wish I was there to comfort you.'

'I will try to simmer down.'

'Good, it's not worth replaying it in your mind.'

'Okay Dr. Sharvin, I will try. So you say everything is going well in Amsterdam?'

'Yes, it has been an interesting one this time around. It's over tomorrow and then I get to see a few sights and take in the experience. Hang in there, wish you were here too. I'll call you soon or you call me when you need an ear. One week to go.'

Grace hung up, sat on the edge of the bed and thought about the news of Felicity's hasty, clandestine marriage. She knew Patience would not be given any reasons for her decision or an explanation on how she met the journalist.

Felicity was a woman of her own making, her difficult entry into the world, made her hard and private, yet she was the most giving person they knew, outside their own little family. She believed that time would melt away this momentary impasse.

Friendships based on mutual respect, and accepting that privacy and space are necessary to preserve the longevity of the friendship, is not negotiable. This resonated with Grace in her relationship with Patience.

*   *   *

The social culture of Amsterdam was appealing, privacy and the 'live and let live' attitude had her thinking that living in Amsterdam would suit her own needs and personality. While there appeared to be a distant, aloof manner she encountered in public spaces, she felt the warmth Nina exuded. The directness of the people and nuances of language reminded Grace of Afrikaner culture and lifestyle in South Africa. Her thoughts went back to Anton Wessels who showed tremendous respect for her mother. She wondered what had become of him. She felt guilty for not making the effort to stay in touch and decided to look him up when she returned to Australia.

Nina called to confirm the dinner date at her home.

Grace accepted and Keefe Daly was invited to join them.

In her brief time in Amsterdam, Grace noted the lack of pretentiousness and absence of materialism, cars were not given prestige, bicycles were the convenient mode of transportation, and homes were a private domicile with very few invitations extended to dine in people's homes. Dinner table conversations were either professional or simple. Grace remembered her mother's bone of contention while living in South Africa, where the competitive edge for some was palpable while poverty flourished for the majority. Varuna condemned such an attitude but offered that she understood how apartheid had encouraged destructive socio-economic elitism where people sought acknowledgement from an excessive show of materialistic wealth.

Nina's hallway was adorned with fresh tulips grown in green houses during winter. A life-size effigy of *Sinterklaas* took pride of place in the living room to delight young Finn. Each time he squeezed *Sinterklaas'* hand, a robust *Ho! Ho! Ho! Vrolijk Kerstfeest* was belted out. The fireplace was cosy and inviting with a fire that sat low in the grate, creating a genial atmosphere.

Grace was impressed with Keefe's interest in food, its history, flavours, herbs, and spices. She thought, Patience would get on well with him, they shared a passion for food. It was time she told her sister about the man she had met, the charming Dr. Keefe Daly, with his endearing accent, a good crop of hair, beginning to grey around the temples and warm, attentive manner.

Nina asked Grace, 'what was the highlight of your touring, Grace? I know you've got two days before you head home so there may be more experiences that will yet delight you.'

'Well, I love *Soezen*' Grace laughed.

'You say that like it's a place, instead of a profiterole!'

'I have had one too many of them and plan to bake them too when I get home. But, to be honest, I love the unobtrusive nature of the people, they are friendly when approached but inhabit their own social spaces.'

'This is true, that is why living and studying in England was not too different for me, I think.'

Keefe listened with a smile, nodding in agreement as he settled down to a glass of port with Nina's husband.

'Lovely of you to have me over Nina, I hope you will visit me in Australia someday.'

'We would love to, but not for another few years, perhaps when Finn is a little older.'

'I hope we stay in touch and I see you when you decide to make that trip.'

Keefe and Grace left Nina and her delightful family around 11 p. m. He suggested they have a night cap in the hotel lounge bar before they retired for the night. She welcomed the idea with nervous excitement.

He confirmed he was accepting the two year contract in Australia. This bit of news delighted her.

She could not help thinking Nina might be right about their mutual attraction.

32

Secrets Shared

Grace's departure from Amsterdam left her nostalgic. She formed friendships and enjoyed being around people who were not quick to probe and pry into her life. Nina's effervescent personality created a yearning to sustain the friendship that developed between them.

Patience's unexpected decision to pick her up from the airport and whiz her off for a home cooked meal and the surprise of two new additions to their family made it a special homecoming.

Ajax and Sprite bounded from the back of the house, jumping on Grace, almost knocking her off her feet.

'Oh my goodness! Who do we have here? When did you get these adorable babies?'

'I got them just after you left, but wanted to surprise you. I put them out in the yard each time I called you, lest these fellas snorted or barked, letting out my secret.' Her warm, husky laugh as she clapped her hands with joy at her well-kept secret, had Grace laughing too.

'They were abandoned in an old building on the south side of town. I could not take one and leave the other behind. They are high maintenance in the love department but adorable to come home to.'

She felt the sting of loneliness in Patience's words, and avoided saying anything about meeting Keefe.

'You should get some help to maintain them, your work life is hectic enough. I'm happy to look after them for you, on my days off.'

'Thanks, Grace, I might just call on *Aunty Grace* to look after my babies. You must have a lot to tell me about your trip.'

'*Aunty Grace* makes me feel warm and fuzzy,' she laughed, 'I'll fill you in later. How are things between you and Felicity these days?'

'I think we are better this week, I've let it go and I am now helping her arrange the reception dinner. She wants it themed and wait for it... she wants the Academy Awards theme to showcase both hers and Refalo's favourite movies! They are both avid moviegoers. There's the attraction, I think!'

Grace was relieved to hear Patience laughing. She had thawed from her initial disappointment of being left out in the cold in her best friend's important, life-changing decision. Life lessons, friendships tested, happen at any stage of life, this made her reconsider whether overzealousness in friendships should be tempered. While friendships wax and wane, Patience knew that her love and loyalty were steadfast. She was Varuna's and Elsie's daughter, they respected unquestioning trust and loyalty.

'Well, yes some are movie lover couples and some are dog lover couples. We have to find you a dog lover soon.'

Patience cringed, then smiled before responding, not wanting to crush Grace's refreshing, newfound joy.

'Yeah, I suppose when the time is right. You were going to tell me something when you called from Amsterdam before I bombarded you with my Felicity grief, I'm dying to hear your news.'

'It's not all that exciting, the lovely Nina Holstead, a member of the hosting committee, invited me to a meal at her home before I left.'

'It must make a big difference going on these international conferences and meeting someone who extends a kind hand of friendship.'

'This was by far the best I've attended. I met a lovely Irish doctor too, Keefe Daly who will be working in Australia soon.'

'I'm really glad you were able to meet a few good people, what field is he in?'

'He runs an ER facility in Belfast, he's coming out here on a two year contract soon. He jokingly said the weather attracted him and that was the sole reason for accepting the contract.'

'He sounds like fun, not those typically stuffed shirts that look down their noses at each other. Phew, I remember such folk when I came along as your guest, to your last conference dinner. Snobs!'

'Yes, he is down to earth and a foodie! He wants to know about the ingredients in everything he eats so I think you two will get on quite well.'

'Oh, you got to know him on an intimate level, I take it?' Patience's curious brow and sudden formal tone had Grace wondering how she would react if she told her she was attracted to the Irishman.

'Not intimate, he's Nina Holstead's family friend and we met at her place again for dinner and ended up having drinks at the hotel later that evening.'

Patience smiled her mischievous smile which Grace knew meant she had cottoned on to her 'connection' with Keefe.

'Aah, I do believe I hear the flutter of your stolen heart, my sister! I will have to give him the once over with my beady eye first, before you give all of your heart away if you haven't already done so!'

'Not at all, he's a lovely man and I will introduce him around when he arrives in a few months, help him settle in.'

'You've said 'lovely man', a fair few times, so no plans to settle down with him, then?' Patience resumed her fun-filled girlish *wanting-to-know-more* glint in her eye attitude. She was not going to let Grace get away with dregs of information, she wanted to know everything! Nothing was too much information on matters of the heart.

'Stop it Patience, I only met him two weeks ago and there was no hanky-panky!'

'Aha! I have a feeling I should be prepared for anything after the stunt Felicity pulled!'

'I won't be pulling any such stunts, you can be assured of that.'

'Time will tell! If I recall you did not like 'white boys'. I remember the besotted Anton Wessels, poor guy, it's been ages since we last heard from him.'

'It had nothing to do with 'white boys,' my studying was my priority and besides I didn't like his game-ranger look! What about you? You were secretive about any of your love interests. Strange that you should mention Anton Wessels, I had a fleeting thought about where he was and how he was doing.'

'We should search for him on Facebook and get in touch again, to honour Mama Varuna's respect for him. And, on the subject of secrets, I have a few. One secret you would never have guessed and neither would anyone else nor the person in question, so here it is — I had a massive crush on Petros Sibaya. I don't think he felt the same way about me.'

'Patience! How could you have kept this from me? I had no idea! You hid it well. That's just as bad as what Felicity did. Did you tell Petros how you felt?'

'No, way! Are you crazy? He was a proud Zulu man. Can you imagine me doing that?'

'I think he loved you. Who would go to the lengths he did, putting his own life at risk, to bring you safely home from the chief's den.'

'That was indeed a self-sacrificing gesture which claimed his life, I live with it every day. He was loyal to Mama Varuna, too, and would do anything to help her.'

Grace looked at Patience, seeing the ghosts she carried from their lives in South Africa, revisited in her eyes.

'It was something you could not have prevented, the very nature of the political landscape made life cheap there. Look at our own fathers and what happened to them. Nobody is to blame but the one committing the crime.'

'I wish I could see it that way,' she sighed, 'anyway, Virginia Bale is taking on more hours at the ladies' centre. This makes it possible for me to take some time out soon.'

'I'm so glad to hear that, you need a long vacation to an exotic land to meet new and exciting people.'

Patience did not let the moment slip in Grace's last line, 'like a certain Dr. Keefe Daly?'

*   *   *

Felicity's wedding reception was everything she wanted it to be. Alf Refalo, thirty years her senior, was the happiest man alive, Felicity was his attentive and caring bride.

The Academy Awards theme, from lighting, costumes, the red carpet, make-believe television reporters and movie excerpts playing on large screens, was spectacular. After dinner, lucky draws were held for the best dressed and partners were given 'best supporting role' prizes. Many were invited to give an acceptance speech after reciting selected lines from their favourite movies. The evening was a theme-park extravaganza, no expense was spared.

Felicity brought all her childhood hopes and dreams to fruition on this night. She came in dressed as Queen Victoria and dressed Alf Refalo as Jack Sparrow. In that coupled combination, she was role-playing the essence of her life, the desire to be someone of note and having to live by fighting her way through life. Felicity, bold and courageous, was not going to let anything stand in her way of happiness. Grace studied the couple, Felicity appeared as a child being indulged by her wealthy father. Her choice

to be with an almost incapacitated, aging man after her childhood years, facing constant abuse by multiple men in multiple foster homes led to this indulgent, yet somewhat perceived 'safe' relationship. Was she seeking a father figure in her life? This thought saddened Grace. Felicity was a beautiful, graceful woman with the kindest heart given to occasions when her tongue got the better of her, but, she was a good woman. She was happy that Patience had mended their momentary rift. All three women were a united force to be reckoned with. Partners who committed to them would be lucky to be loved by them. Husbands or partners of Grace, Patience or Felicity would have to have strong feminist views if they had an iota of hope of being loved in return.

Grace noted with quiet joy, Virginia's glowing presence in her blue and silver cocktail dress and flowing mane of healthy, shiny hair. She was on the road to her brighter future. Assisting Virginia is what her mother would have expected of her. Was this her pardoning for harbouring a secret from her loving mother?

*   *   *

Lots transpired in the months after Felicity's marriage. She was occupied with caring for Alf and assisted Patience whenever she could while continuing her mission on alleviating the refugee crisis. Virginia worked full-time with Patience, she was preparing for her first speaking engagement in Perth. Keefe Daly flew in for a week from Belfast to sign off his contract. As Grace predicted, Keefe and Patience got on like a house on fire. He was due back in six weeks to begin his contract in Sydney.

Grace went over to spend the night with Patience who did not stay over at Grace's these days, taking on a maternal role with Ajax and Sprite. After a few glasses of wine, Patience revved up the courage to reveal what Grace was not expecting to hear.

'I've been thinking a lot lately that I would like to take a long trip to South Africa.'

Grace tried to conceal her surprise. Patience maintained she would never go back to bitter memories.

'Do you mean that or is this the wine talking,' Grace laughed.

'I'm being very serious. Recently, I've been thinking about my birth culture and my heritage. I must be getting old because I've never felt like this before. I want to look for the people from Mama Elsie's tribe, I want to know more about my ancestry and my parents' lives.'

Grace listened, not quite believing what she was hearing, not sure for the first time if it was her place to deter Patience from such yearnings.

'Don't look so sad Grace, I will be back, my work here is important to me. I need some confirmation after all these years that I am an authentic woman. You are my sister for life, I just need the cultural connection for a period, a sort of pilgrimage.'

'I get what you're saying, you have memories of a culture that was taken from you when you came to live with us, and we are wired to seek that connection when we move away from it. I do understand Patience, but I will be terrified for your safety.'

'I've thought about that, I will be a tourist this time, and will take necessary precautions. Nobody will be looking for me to be any chief's wife. I will be considered soiled goods now, not a sought-after good wife — more a tainted whore.' she laughed as she sucked in her cheeks and screwed up her face.

'You are not tainted, tribal thinking is corrosive enough to put you in that ridiculous category!'

'There's more, I'm sorry to spill this all at once. I have given this tremendous thought. There are many sisters who are destitute there, I have been in touch with an organisation that is prepared to assist with setting up safe houses in South Africa, in the areas of greatest need.' Grace studied Patience's body language, she looked peaceful speaking her truth.

'You are my family, my only family, I will not forsake you, Grace. Now is the time for me, with Virginia taking the reins, to explore what my heart yearns. She will stay at my house and I've told her, her grandmother is welcome to stay there with her and Sprite and Ajax will be well taken care of in my absence.'

'You have thought it all through. How long will you be away? Is it for a year?' She tried to avoid sounding selfish. As much as her own heart protested, she felt the heartbeat of her sister's desire to rub shoulders, for a while, with her people.

'I have more news, its best I tell you everything now, there should not be any holding back between us ever again. I applied for a once in a lifetime venture which I plan to take up after spending three months in South Africa… I will be away for six months.'

'May I know what this venture is?' Grace felt dread beginning to grip her senses.

'This organisation is holding a three month training on global trends in social justice initiatives, covering all aspects that need addressing as a global network. Those trained will then form a satellite network to contribute to human progress in selected locations.'

'Is this a United Nations initiative? You have done your homework on this, I gather. It must cost you a fortune to join this crusade.'

'No it's a private enterprise. On the contrary, all I have to pay is the airfare. A flight of internationally selected delegates leaves from Singapore to a venue in Thailand. It's an amazing place which in part will be an extended holiday too.'

'How did you find this amazing opportunity?' Grace felt uneasy about Patience going into the unknown.

'I received an email saying my work came to their attention and this offer was available to develop and grow what I'm doing. Seems like I was destined for this.'

As Varuna's daughter, Grace remembered her mother's words, *live and let live, we were born free. We must be patient, what we love, will return after a period of absence.* Varuna's intense optimism and wisdom lingered but Grace could not still her fear. She had to support her sister as she was always supported by her.

*   *   *

On the last day of June, an uneasy Grace waved Patience off at the airport for her six month sojourn. She said a silent prayer for her safe return and the blessing of attaining the spiritual elevation she craved. She understood Patience's need – as much as the country was consumed by corruptive politics and waves of crime, the spirit of the people in their birthplace was an undeniable tug, a heartbeat that was never quite stilled. Mama Elsie's quiet, spiritual aura and a beautiful smile warmed any troubled child. Grace felt the emptiness, as she too yearned for the soil she once called home. Patience needed this time for mature contemplation and the opportunity to embrace what was to extend her life calling. So much had changed in their lives in the last six months.

Grace had a three hour wait at the airport, Dr. Keefe Daly was arriving from Ireland to begin his medical contract in Australia.

Entrances and exits are necessary as the voices of the heart beckon a changing or reshaping of what lies ahead.

235

The wound is the place where the light enters you
~ Rumi

Also by Mala Naidoo

Would you risk your long held dreams for a secluded estate beside an olive grove, a creative paradise, and a mysterious, irresistible newcomer? Set in London and Florence with a third location being 'any place' Meryl, a budding writer, and Michael a human rights lawyer, become entangled in the world of international crime. Life will never be quite the same. Will they pick up from where they left, despite the various characters who managed to enter their lives, or will they let go of the safety they once found in each other's arms?

A contemporary story of fractured pasts, intriguing encounters, insularity, professional harassment and the capacity to live for others.

Published by Sid Harta Publishers.

Vindication Across Time, the sequel to *Across Time and Space*, exposes how too much power corrupts the very establishments society is called upon to trust and obey. As the wheels of deception slowly untangle, those who were once maligned are vindicated while those who were trusted, face a dark future.

A tale of love and loss, where the choices made, lead Meryl and Andrei down a path they both had not imagined.

Website: www.malanaidoo.com

www.ingramcontent.com/pod-product-compliance
Lightning Source LLC
Chambersburg PA
CBHW030639110726
47901CB00002B/500